UNDENIABLE

Indulgence series

A NOVELLA

Aleatha Romig
New York Times, Wall Street Journal, and USA Today
bestseller

COPYRIGHT AND LICENSE INFORMATION

UNDENIABLE

Indulgence series

A NOVELLA

2020 Edition License

BLURB

UNDENIABLE

Indulgence series A NOVELLA

Forbidden love...is undeniable.

When she was younger, like all little girls, Sophie Hawkins believed in fantasies. She believed in happily-ever-after and that one day her prince would come. What made Sophie's dreams a bit different was that the man of her dreams wasn't a fictional prince but her best friend's dad.

Matt was handsome and nice, the kind of man every woman would want.

Time passes, and through the years, Sophie's reality changes, yet her attraction and memories of Matt Hamilton never fade. Where boys and men are concerned, Matt remains her gold standard.

When his daughter was young, Matt Hamilton had it all: a family and success.

With the ticking of the clock and changing of the calendar, seasons pass and situations adjust. Business success remains, but personally, his world changes...until the day fate sets the undeniable in motion.

Sophie was a sweet little girl, his daughter's best friend, and a ray of undeniable sunshine. That was before. Now she's more. She is a grown woman.

Who can deny the undeniable?
Have you been Aleatha'd?

Undeniable, part of the *Indulgence series* of stand-alone steamy stories, will heat your ereader and make you hot and bothered. Undeniable is a fun forbidden-love story that will whisk the reader away to a time when fantasies could come true.

DEDICATION

To everyone who never stopped believing in fantasies.

PROLOGUE

Sophie:

Years ago

*a*s the waves crash over the sand and shells, my eyes go to the man standing thigh deep in the water. I hold my breath as the ocean laps around his legs, each wave licking the hem of his bathing suit. He's solid and unmoving as he stands watching over the sea. The salt-filled breeze blows his dark hair away from his face, revealing handsome features that I can't even begin to describe.

His eyes are covered with sunglasses, yet I know their color—green like his daughter's, like my best friend's.

I don't understand his mood. It's as if he isn't watching a beautiful scene, as if he's a million miles away instead of on the beach in the most amazing place I've ever been. I can't keep my eyes off of him though I know it's wrong. I'm too young to understand this kind of attraction, yet I'm drawn to him.

I try to think of stories.

Is it the way Cinderella felt when she saw Prince Charming for the first time?

Jasmine, when she saw Aladdin?

Maybe it's more like Belle when she met the beast.

Mr. Hamilton isn't scary like the beast; however, there is something about the way I feel when I'm around him that makes me feel off-balance.

He isn't like the boys at Becky's and my school. He isn't a boy. He's a man, and for the first time that I can remember, I wish I were a woman. Though it doesn't matter. He doesn't even notice me. Why would he? I'm just a little girl, his daughter's friend.

It's not as if I'm trying to feel different around him—I don't want to. After all, he's my best friend's dad. But Mr. Hamilton doesn't look like a dad—not like my dad. My dad wears dark socks with his shorts and sandals. His legs are pale from working inside all the time. My dad tells stupid jokes and then laughs when no one else does.

That's what dads do.

Becky's dad doesn't do any of those things.

Shaking my head, I do my best to tuck the feelings away.

No matter what we try, some memories never go away.

SOPHIE

J brush the lint from my black top and skirt. It's the same outfit I wear when I'm working at the Ritz's upscale restaurant. Since event planning is my intended major, a teacher at my high school thought it would be a good idea to get some practical experience, plus she knew I needed the money.

It must have worked because I'm starting university in less than a month.

Though my grandparents are helping with my expenses, every little bit of extra money is a plus. That's why, after a one-to-six shift at the Ritz, I agreed to work this private dinner party. After all, private parties are events. My boss, Cindy, did the planning, but she's been great about letting me help with the organization.

I was a little surprised when she asked me to help with this event—it isn't that large. But once I was here at this beautiful home, I was very glad she did.

Now, at a little after midnight, absolutely dead on my feet and ready to slip out of these three-inch black heels, I can finally take a satisfied deep breath.

"Good job, Sophie," Cindy says. "I knew when Mr. Hamilton asked for you, you'd do a great job."

My tired mind deciphers her words. "What? He asked for me? You didn't tell me that."

She grins. "I didn't need to. You said yes when I asked." She pats my shoulder. "Go on and go home. You have to be beat. Everything is wrapped up here. Do you need a ride?"

I let my gaze move to the large windows overlooking the pool and deck. Imagining my grandparents' house, all stuffy and covered in doilies, I long for the fresh air and sea breeze. "I should take a ride, but I think first I'll make sure everything is put away out on the deck, and then I'll call an Uber."

"Are you sure? I don't mind driving you."

I know my grandparents' home is out of her way, and she is just being nice.

"I'm good," I say with a smile. I really should buy a car, but I can't spare the cash. I need every cent for university and expenses. Since my parents died and I moved in with my grandparents, they have done their best. My grandpa even lets me drive his car, but it isn't right to leave them without one. I mean, they're old.

What if something happened?

"Here." Cindy slips me a roll of cash, and my eyes

open wide. I can't tell how much it is, but unless the bills are singles, it's more than I ever expected.

She wraps her hand around mine. "It's your share of tips. It'll help you with that Uber."

"Thank you."

"No, thank you. You're a natural at this party stuff. After you graduate from university, maybe I can work for you."

My cheeks lift higher, and I tilt my head. "Or you could hire me full time?"

Cindy winks. "See you later."

As I walk toward the open door, I feel that satisfied contentment of a job well done. The party went off without a hitch. Since I spent most of my time making sure the servers were doing their jobs and the cleaners were picking up the used glasses, plates, and silverware, I didn't get a chance to truly appreciate the home.

Mr. Hamilton's home.

When I was young—okay, a child—I had a friend whose last name was Hamilton. Becky Hamilton. Though I hadn't really gotten a chance to meet this Mr. Hamilton, I know he can't be the same one as Becky's father. Becky and I grew up in a solid everyday neighborhood with hardworking parents. They could never afford a place like this. Besides, Hamilton is a common name. Heck, it's even the title of a Broadway musical.

Though Becky and I lost touch after I moved in with

my grandparents, the thing I remember the most about Becky's family is her dad. I actually feel my heart clench at the memories. He was the dad that all the girls in the neighborhood lusted after.

Maybe we didn't lust. I mean, do eight-year-olds lust? Just hearing the name *Hamilton* reminds me of how much I liked him. It isn't something a girl forgets. It is his image that comes to mind, the one from my memories, that I see in my dreams, the ones where I wake with my fingers in my folds and rubbing my clit.

I know I'll probably never see him again, and besides, he's married, or he was. But for me he'll always be the gold standard. I will probably die a virgin because no one will ever be Matt Hamilton.

Slipping out to the pool deck, I sigh, looking up at the multitude of sparkling stars.

I can't imagine living in a house like this one. It isn't that my grandparents are poor—they aren't—but this is beyond my comprehension. The pool deck extends all the way to the edge of the bay. I'm sure it has a name—all the bodies of water do—but not a name most people would know. Even this piece of the ocean is private, only accessible to the few homes that grace its shores.

I smile as the warm breeze blows the palm tree's fronds above my head. With only the faint-colored lights beneath the pool's water and what is shining through the large windows from the house, it's like the pool is a haven of peace. After the number of people who were served inside the house and out on the deck, the current solitude definitely is.

It is with this little slice of freedom that I can't resist one last look at the property.

I'm about to sink onto one of the cushioned chairs when a deep voice startles me.

"Are you enjoying yourself?"

My heart rate accelerates as I turn toward the voice. In the dimness, I can't make out all of the man's features, but I can tell he's tall with broad shoulders. His hair appears dark, and as he nears, so do his eyes, although there is a flash of green. Maybe it's the reflection of the pool's lights.

"I-I'm sorry. I'm about to call for my ride," I say as I fumble for my phone in my purse.

The man steps closer, and I wonder if he could be the host. As he nears, I take in his attire. The party was formal, and he's wearing a tuxedo. The tie is now loosened, and I can't stop my grin. It's a real tie, one he had to actually tie into a bow, not the clip kind boys my age would wear to a dance.

"It's beautiful. Isn't it?" His voice fades into the sound of the soft waves on the shore as he stands with one hand in his pocket, looking out over the bay.

Following his gaze, I nod. "It is. I would never tire of this as my backyard."

His laugh rumbles, sending vibrations to my core. For only a moment I'm afraid he's making fun of me, but then he turns and extends his hand.

"Hardly a yard. The water is paradise. Come see. There's a manatee getting closer."

I do as he says. As his fingers encase mine, my steps momentarily stutter. There's something in his touch, warmth that shoots through me from my fingers to my toes. It's like electricity.

Shyly I raise my eyes to his, wondering if he feels it too.

Instead of confirming or denying, he pulls me closer to the edge of the stone decking. Without letting go of my hand, he points with his other. "Look. See the ripples?"

"I do!" I keep my excitement to a stage whisper.

The water moves. The rays of moonlight no longer reflect, showcasing the large water mammal.

"Oh, it's so big!"

He turns toward me with a lopsided grin. "Words to a man's heart."

I fight to pull my hand away, knowing that pink is filling my cheeks. "I meant the manatee. If I hadn't lived the last eight years in Florida, I would be petrified with one so close."

He releases my hand and casually wraps his arm around my shoulder. "Then I wish you were new to the area."

I try to swallow as I turn within his grasp, facing him. "You do?"

"Yes, then you would be a damsel in distress, and I could protect you."

"A true knight in shining armor?"

His embrace of my shoulders lowers to the small of my back as he pulls me closer. "No, Sophie Hawkins, I'm not a knight."

SOPHIE

"*W*ait. How do you know my name?"

My heart pounds against the buttons of his tuxedo as he brings my breasts crashing against his chest. "Because I've known you for most of your life. I've been waiting all night to get you alone."

I stare up at his handsome face. I must be dreaming. Maybe it's my mind—I'm tired. I need sleep.

"How?"

He holds me out to arm's length. "Look at me, Sophie, with those gorgeous blue eyes you had even as a child. Look at me. Tell me you don't know me."

My lips disappear behind my teeth as I do as he says. The moon combined with the light streaming from the windows creates the only illumination as I stare up at Mr. Hamilton—dark hair and green eyes.

He can't be the man in my memories, the one I've fantasized about. He'd be older now. This man doesn't seem older, not really. He is as sexy and dominating as I remember, even more so. His presence consumes me. I feel small in his embrace but not young. The pulsating between my legs tells me that I feel nothing like the child who used to idolize him. I'm a woman, a woman who wants my fantasies to become reality.

"M-Mr. Hamilton? Matt Hamilton?"

His lips move upward, revealing his million-dollar smile. As I gaze up into his handsome face, my body relaxes against his, fluid in his grasp, while conversely his hardens, his erection probing my stomach.

I've never been with a man, nothing more than heavy petting. They all paled in comparison to my fantasies, but by the way my body is reacting, it knows the truth my mind has just begun to accept.

This is Matt Hamilton, and he is my fantasy.

My face inclines toward his. "How? Why?"

Before he answers, one of his hands captures my neck and pulls me the few inches closer until our lips connect.

Heat radiates from our kiss like lightning flashing through me, igniting streaks of fire from my lips to my toes and back again. It's like no kiss I've ever had. Matt takes and gives without concern for the future.

Here, now. It's all that matters as I moan while simultaneously catching my breath.

"I've dreamt about this," I manage to say. "Maybe I'm dreaming?"

The hand from my neck moves possessively down my

side, skimming the side of my breast. His touch is fire that doesn't burn but smolders.

"Oh!"

This isn't a dream. Every nerve in my body is suddenly alive, and I want more. Maybe it is only one night, a fantasy, but as I squeeze my thighs together, I know that without a doubt, I want Matt Hamilton to be my first.

And then I remember my childhood friend.

I take a painful step away from him, backing away from my every dream. "What about your wife?"

He shakes his head. "We've been divorced for over five years."

"So you're not...you're not married?"

"I haven't been for a while, but I'd like to be."

"Is there someone...someone you're seeing?" I ask.

"I am seeing someone. I'd like to see more of her." His smile grows. "I'm looking at her right now."

MATT

I can't believe Sophie is really here. I know people might think my obsession with her is wrong, but it isn't. I've been divorced for five years and she's an adult. She's eighteen, and I can't deny my need to make her mine.

She entered my heart as a child, a beautiful, fun-loving child. She was always so happy and upbeat. I loved the breath of fresh air she brought to our home. Her presence did more than make Becky happy; it lightened everyone around her.

Becky's mother and I went through our problems— we even tried counseling with a sex therapist, Dr. Kizer —and over time, I forgot about the sweet little girl with the big blue eyes. I moved on with my life and my business. Things went well with business. It dominated my world. I've been extremely successful.

My personal life side not so much.

And then I stumbled across something about Sophie on one of my daughter's Facebook memories. I dug a little more and learned about the loss of Sophie's parents and her struggles. It broke my heart to think of the carefree happy girl being sad.

I watched from afar. At first, my goal was to help her financially. Obviously, she's working too much for someone so young. I never see pictures of her out having fun like others her age. Instead, her posts are about school and work, too much for someone so young. Then as she matured, I longed to see a carefree woman, an older version of the little girl.

Now, the way she's looking at me, I can only hope that she hasn't forgotten me or doesn't think of me as some old man.

The thickest, longest lashes I've ever seen veil her big blue eyes as she lowers her chin. "Please don't tease me because I've thought of you often."

She's thought of me?

Immediately, I miss her eyes, so I lift her chin. "Sophie, the only teasing I want to do to you has nothing to do with who I'm seeing. I know this may sound like I'm some sort of creep, but I never forgot you, your smile, or your laugh. I lost track of you, but then a few years ago you popped up on Facebook, and I learned what you've been going through. I'm amazed by the woman you are, even though you're young."

Her chest expands and contracts, pressing her tits against my chest, making my dick grow harder as I imagine feeling them against my skin. I envision their perkiness as her nipples harden at my touch. Fuck that, at my words, as I tell her what I want to do to her.

"Young?" she asks in almost a whisper. "You think I'm too young?"

"I think you're perfect. I think you're old enough to decide if you want to see me—to be with me—and if you want me to see you."

"Y-you'd want that? To see me?"

Her innocence captivates me. There's a sparkle in her shy grin. I want to take away that shyness—and be the one to take her innocence. I want her to feel more comfortable with me than she ever has with anyone else.

I lower my lips to hers, wanting to go slow, but the attraction is too strong. I can't simply brush a chaste kiss on her. I need to have her: her lips, her soft skin, all of her. There's not an inch of her I don't want to claim. My cock turns to stone as I imagine having all of her: her small tits in the palms of my hands and my cock buried deep inside her.

All at once I wonder.

Is Facebook right?

Or could she be seeing someone else?

Has someone else had what I want as mine?

I force our kiss to end as I look down at her veiled eyes and bruised lips. "Tell me. Tell me the truth. Are you seeing someone?"

She doesn't speak, but her head moves from side to side.

Though I'm relieved, I need to know one more thing. I know it sounds shitty, like some sort of barbaric caveman, but I want to know. "Have you? Has someone else been with you?"

Her head falls forward until her forehead hits my chest. I sense sadness emanating from her. The silence eats at me like acid in my gut, filling me with a fury that I can't describe. I haven't seen Sophie in years, yet I've known the undeniable truth for a while—she is mine.

Should I have moved sooner?

Did someone else touch her?

Did someone hurt her?

Fuck! Her dad is gone. Who has protected her?

I'm not a violent man, but as the silence settles over us, my fists clench, wanting to hurt whoever's hurt her. Why would someone have this amazing woman in their arms, take her most prized possession, and leave her?

"Tell me," I growl.

"No." Her voice is again soft. "I've never...I'm a virgin." She looks up. "I'm sorry if that makes me seem like a child, if that makes you not want me. I'm not experienced like the women you're probably used to."

The relief is intoxicating. I pull her closer, my dick aching to take away that title, not just once but for the rest of our lives. "No." I caress her cheek with my now-relaxed knuckles. "It doesn't make you seem like a child. It makes you seem like a gift. My gift."

She nods. "I want to be yours. I've never had sex, but I've thought about it, fantasized about it."

My mind goes to the sex therapist I saw years ago and how she encouraged exploration of fantasies. While her advice didn't change the downward spiral of my first marriage, the meaning resonates with me. Maybe it wasn't the advice but my partner.

The tip of my dick moistens, and I hesitate with my next question. As it is, I'm about to come just by rubbing against her. If I add thinking about her fantasies, surely, I'll blow. I can't help myself. "Do you ever touch yourself when you think about it—when you fantasize?"

The shyness from before lessens as she meets me eye to eye. "Yes, and believe it or not, you're the one in my fantasies."

Fuck!

My eyes open wider. "Me? Why me?"

"Because" —she reaches for my cock and rubs— "I remember you. I've never wanted a boy. I've dreamt of a man, a man who will teach me and show me. I've fantasized about you. It was probably wrong, but you were always the man of my dreams."

I reach for her hand. I do it because I like the feel of it in mine but also because I'm about to shoot my load right here, right now. If she keeps rubbing my dick, it will be over before it starts, and that's not exactly the manly thing to do.

"I want to take you inside the house and make you mine." I kiss her knuckles. "But if I do, you need to understand that this isn't a one-and-done deal. I'm not that kind of man. I've been patiently waiting. I've watched you. I remember your smile and carefree air. I remember how you brought the sun with you everywhere you went. I want to see that in your eyes again. Sophie, if I fuck you tonight, you'll be mine forever."

She doesn't speak, looking at where our hands are intertwined. And then only her eyes move to mine. "Take me, Matt. Help me remember what it's like to feel good."

SOPHIE

*a*s Matt takes my hand and leads me through his house, I fight the feeling that it is all a dream. His hand is warm and possessive. The scent of his cologne fills my nose with spice and the perfect amount of pine and musk. It's manly yet not overpowering. His broad shoulders are right in front of me, wider than I remembered, wider than any of the boys from my high school. I can still taste his kiss, sweet with a hint of alcohol, something strong and intoxicating. And I hear his shoes upon the marble steps as we move up the huge staircase. Yet I feel as though I'm floating. His feet are hitting the floor, but I have to look down to be sure mine are too.

How can this be happening to me?

Before I can overthink it, Matt opens two large doors to the biggest bedroom I've ever seen. The king-sized bed seems small in comparison. One wall is filled with windows, and in the windows is a door leading to a balcony overlooking the bay. As he releases my hand and walks toward the windows, I turn a full circle, taking in the woodwork and custom artistry. I've never seen such understated luxury.

"Matt?"

He stills as he reaches for a switch. "Yes?"

"Is this real?"

He pushes a switch causing the windows to change to an opaque shade. Though there are no curtains, I'm certain that what he did closed out the outside world, making this just about us.

My breathing hitches as he turns. Each step toward me is predatory, like a jungle beast about to capture his prey. And though I know I'm the prey, I'm not frightened. I want to show him that I'm ready for my fantasies to come true. Bravely, I take one step and then another, meeting him halfway.

"This is real." He reaches for my hand and rubs it over his steel-hard erection. "And so is this, and it needs to be inside you. It needs to find its new home."

My thighs squeeze tight at his words as my core throbs, craving what he describes. At the same time, a part of me is beginning to get nervous. His cock feels so big to my touch. Maybe he won't fit. Maybe I am too young. "I-I," I stutter as my daring facade shatters.

Matt reaches for my cheek and tenderly teases my skin. "Sophie, I promise to make it good. I want you to want my cock inside of you as much as I want it there. I'll take this as slow and gentle as you want."

My fantasies come back to mind, scenes from books I've read. "What if I don't want that?"

He takes a small step back. "You don't want this?"

I reach for the lapels of his jacket and push them over his wide shoulders, purposely running my fingers over his starched shirt, imagining his solid muscles beneath. "No. I want this. What if I don't want you to be slow and gentle?"

Before he can answer, I go on. "What if I want you to take me fast and hard?"

"Sophie?"

"Matt, you're the man of my dreams. In those dreams, you take control and claim me. Is this real life, or is it my dream?"

"Fuck!" He reaches for the waistband of my skirt, undoes the button, and lowers the zipper allowing the material to float to the floor, creating a black puddle around my heels.

As he does, I reach for my shirt and pull it over my head.

Suddenly I'm standing in front of Matt Hamilton in nothing but black heels, a black bra, and polka-dotted panties.

So much for sexy.

"I'm sorry I'm not wearing some Victoria's Secret lacy thing."

Matt's smile broadens as he runs his hand from my

neck over my boobs and down my stomach, teasing the edge of my panties.

"I'm going to say this once, and you'd better listen."

There's something about his voice. It's different, authoritative, and makes my heart beat faster.

He cups my chin. "Tell me, beautiful Sophie, are you listening?"

"Yes."

"That was the last time I want to hear you apologize. You're fucking perfect. I'll buy you a closet full of Victoria's Secret if that's what you want, but for me, I want you." He reaches behind me and unsnaps my bra. "And the clothes are just the wrapping. Remember, you're my gift."

"I just don't want you to change your mind."

"Are you fucking kidding me? You're mine. My mind is never going to change."

I sigh, not only hearing his words but also seeing the way his green eyes devour me, eating me up, piece by piece.

He takes a step back and scans my body from my hair to my shoes and back again. "Now, do as I say."

"Okay."

A sexy shimmer shines from his gaze. "Let your hair down and turn around, all the way around, and as you do, shimmy out of that bra. I've been watching you all night, and I'm dying to get a good look at your tits."

My skin prickles with goose bumps as I reach for the clip in my hair. As I pull, my long blonde hair falls in waves over my shoulders. Without the clasp, the straps have fallen to my arms and the bra is loose. I allow it to drop to the floor, revealing my breasts. Pivoting, I make a complete circle. By the time I'm facing him again, my nipples are as hard as pebbles.

With a smirk, he says, "I love the polka dots, but I have more of my gift to unwrap."

In a quick scoop, Matt has me in his arms and is carrying me toward the big bed. I reach for his tie and pull, dropping it to the floor. By the time he lays me on the comforter, I have most of his shirt's buttons undone. His chest is defined, and I can't resist reaching out to touch his muscles.

Slowly, he removes his shirt and unbuckles his belt. Before undoing his slacks, he reaches down and slides my panties over my hips and down my legs. There's a twinkle in his gaze. "The heels are staying on."

I can't help but smile. The shoes were the one thing I wanted to take off. Now they're all I have on.

"Scoot forward until you're on the edge of the bed."

I try not to think about what he's saying. Mostly I'm thinking about his cock. I can see the bulge in his pants and the way it's pushing against the zipper.

"That's it," he says, encouraging my movements.

Before I can process, Matt reaches for my feet and lifts them to the bed, spreading my legs and exposing my most private parts.

For a moment I'm mortified, wanting to apologize for

not being waxed or ready. But then I remember him telling me not to apologize.

"Oh damn, Sophie, you're soaking wet."

"I-is that...?"

My eyes close and my head falls back as he plunges a finger inside of me.

"Oh!" My entire body tenses at the invasion, and then all at once his voice settles over me.

"It's perfect. Relax, beautiful. Open your eyes and look at me."

I do as he says. His gaze flickers between my eyes and my core.

"Do you know how gorgeous your cunt is? Have you ever looked at it?"

"No," I pant. I've felt it, fingered myself. Though that was nothing like what he's doing—the way he's moving in and out. I can't help myself from moving with him, riding his finger—first one and then two. "Oh!"

"It's pink and wet, and getting all the attention. Your clit is jealous." As he is speaking, he rubs my clit and electricity rips through me. The room fills with my whimpers and moans as he continues to work me.

"Play with your tits, Sophie. I want to see you touch yourself."

Immediately my hands move to my breasts, rubbing and squeezing.

"Pinch them."

I do, and at the same time, Matt falls to his knees. I scream in ecstasy as his tongue takes the place of his fingers. It's like nothing I've ever experienced. The intensity is overwhelming as I try to back away, but his grip is unrelenting. It's as his licks turn to nips and bites that I lose control.

Falling back to the mattress, my entire body convulses as he laps my essence.

MATT

*H*er come is the sweetest honey I've ever tasted. With my arm over her hips, Sophie continues to buck as I lick and suck. I could stay here all night with my face buried in her perfect pink pussy if it weren't for my aching dick.

"Shit, Matt. That was...that was..." Sophie's eyes are glazed with the undeniable sparkle that only comes with a remarkable orgasm. Her voice fades away as she searches for the right word.

"Amazing, spectacular, the sweetest come I've ever tasted."

Releasing my pants, I push them down along with my boxers as I fall on top of her. Keeping my weight on my elbows, I climb up her body, kissing her flawless skin as I propel her farther up the mattress.

"Kiss me. I want you to see how great you taste."

I don't know if I expected her to be tentative, but she

isn't. As soon as our lips touch, Sophie's tongue probes my lips, seeking out her own essence. "You like that? You like your come?"

Sophie's face tilts as her brows lift. "I think I'd like yours better."

I lift my hips. My cock is hard as stone and pointing near my belly button. "Sophie, I want to take you. Remember what I said—once we do this, you're mine."

She pulls my face close and licks my chin. "I already am."

Reaching down, I fist my shaft. I'm not sure I've ever been this hard. The tip of my dick is slick from the come that has leaked out. I know her pussy is wet and ready, but I'm still concerned that my size will hurt her.

As I line up my cock with her entrance, Sophie reaches down and strokes it once and then twice.

"Can I see you? You feel so big."

I shake my head. "I am. I'll let you see after we're done. I don't want my size to scare you."

Her fingers try to surround me. "It already does."

"Don't let it. I promised you to make it good."

I watch as she blinks. My cock rubs over her clit and her folds.

"Tell me when you're ready."

"I'm ready."

I ease inside just a little, watching her expression, the way her pretty pink lips form the perfect "O." "It'll be good. First, I need to take what you've saved for me. I'm going to pop your cherry. I'll make it quick."

She nods, her eyes wide in wonder as I kiss her nose. "Breathe for me."

As her tits push toward me, I plunge, deep and fast. Her pussy is so tight, I feel like I'm forcing myself into a condom three sizes too small. She's strangling me, and it's the most painful pleasure I've ever felt. I'm not all the way in when I meet resistance, the cherry she left for me that was mine since I first met her.

Sophie's body tenses as I push through, going where no one has gone before.

I kiss a tear from her cheek. "That was it, Sophie. Now let me make it better."

She doesn't speak, but she doesn't argue as I begin to move. In and out. Slowly, her pussy releases its death grip of my cock. Her come lets me move with ease, and soon she's moving too. Her back arches as her body moves in rhythm with mine.

I take turns between kissing her neck and sucking her tight-beaded nipples while my fingers reach between us and flick her oversensitive clit. Every time I do, small detonations go off as her core muscles twitch. But it isn't until our rhythm increases and both of our breathing labors that I know I have her on the brink of the best orgasm of her life.

"That's it. I want you to come. I want you to come all over me."

A few more thrusts and she does. Again, she's strangling me from within. Wave after wave of contractions. It's more than I can take as I explode.

Years of watching and waiting have built into a never-ending fountain as I fill her with my seed. Her whimpers and my grunts fill the air. We're crazy people as we both come apart.

When I'm finally done, I fall over her, my arms keeping most of my weight off of her.

I smooth her blonde hair away from her face and wait. Slowly, her eyes open.

"That," she says, her voice shaky. "Earlier...but that..."

I don't pull out, loving the way her pussy holds me. "I promised to make it good."

She shakes her head. "You lied."

"What?"

Her small hand reaches to my cheek. "It wasn't good, Matt. It was fucking fantastic."

"You know it's official now. No denying that you're mine?"

"I think I've known that for most of my life. I just didn't believe it would ever happen."

"Sophie, we didn't talk about protection. Are you on the pill? I know some girls take it to regulate..." My words still as her smile fades. "What is it?"

"Is this another time when I can't apologize?"

"Yes. Protection isn't all your responsibility. I knew what the fuck I was doing. Honestly, I want to hear that you're not on the pill. I want to think my baby could be growing inside of you right now."

Her eyes widen as her smile resumes. "You'd want that?"

"Yes, a thousand times yes." And then it's my smile that fades. "Unless you don't?"

Sophie moves her legs, reminding my cock of its warm haven. Her slight shimmy brings it back to life.

"I'd love that," she says. "To be a mom to your baby. After all, I'm yours, right?"

It's amazing that I'm still hard after all of that, but I am. And hearing Sophie admit that she's mine and wants my babies makes me even harder. I rock my hips, sliding my cock out and gently plunging it in and out.

"Only forever," I whisper as I push in and pull out. I've never felt anything like her pussy. It's tight and smooth, like a silk glove. In no time at all, I find our rhythm.

She's so fucking responsive. As I move, Sophie is moving with me, a gentle rocking.

It's then that I remember her fantasy—fast and hard.

"Sharing fantasies demonstrates trust." Dr. Kizer's words come back to me.

Sophie shared hers.

Though it's the last thing I want to do, I pull out. Before Sophie can say anything, I command, "Roll over. Get on your hands and knees."

It seems as though she's about to hesitate when a large smile fills her expression, and she obeys.

I stroke my cock, running my hand up and down. When I look down, I see it's covered in our silky, sticky come. It's then I notice the pink tint, the evidence of Sophie's gift to me. Her virginity is mine. But I want more. I want to be the only one ever to know the heaven of her cunt.

I lean my body over hers, my cock rubbing against her ass as my chest covers her back. With my lips near her ear, I say, "Sophie, you gave me my fantasy. Now it's your turn."

As I sit back, I slap her ass with my hand, and she cries out, more in shock than pain.

I slap her other butt cheek, seeing my bright red handprints and lean over her again. "Real life or fantasy, what will it be?"

She cranes her neck toward me, her long hair hanging to the other shoulder. "Make my fantasies real."

One more slap on her perfect round ass. "Is this too real?"

Her ass shimmies as her knees move farther apart. From my view, I see our come shining on her thighs. I also see by the way her pussy pulsates that she is ready for more, but I want to hear it.

This time I reach for her hair and fist it tightly. Yanking her head backward, again with my lips near her ear, I suck the sensitive skin of her neck. Her whimpers are an aphrodisiac as my cock throbs in my grip. "Don't make me punish you. I asked you a question. Is this too real?"

I have her face pulled upward. Her tits heave as she fights to breathe. "No," she manages.

"No, *Sir*," I correct.

Her pink tongue darts to her lips. "No, Sir. This is perfect real."

Releasing her hair, I grab her hip and line the tip of my cock up with her cunt. Creating suspense, I dip it in and then pull it out, rubbing the tip from her tight hole to her dripping pussy. After a few times, she moves back toward me as her whine of lust fills the room.

I smack her ass, bringing the red back to life. "No. Remember, I'm in control."

"Yes, Sir."

I tease her opening again. "I believe my girl asked for fast and hard. Is that correct?"

"Yes. Oh, please."

"Please?"

"Please, Sir." Her plea so breathy, it drips with unbridled need and desire.

Without restraint I plunge balls deep inside of her. I never would have been able to do that the first time, but now her cunt is ready for me. It's made for me, and I need to have it, have all of her.

Like an animal, I'm primal and unleashed. Carnal instinct and desire overtake me. There is no gentleness. I'm not sure if I've ever taken a woman with this much force, yet as I pound inside of her, as my balls tighten with unrelenting need to claim this woman and fill her with more of my seed, it is as if I'm possessed.

I'm not sure how long we go at it. Time stands still as my cock plummets and my balls bounce off her firm ass. She comes and comes. I feel her shatter and hear her screams of ecstasy, but I don't stop. I don't even slow. Until, finally, the pleasure overtakes me, and relief floods my system. Sex with Sophie is like a drug I have only heard about—the fucking best high in the world. And then my body collapses as my come fills her to overflowing, leaking down her thighs and onto the bed below.

As I pull out, I have the overwhelming fear that I've been too rough. I don't know where it came from, and though it felt right, I am suddenly concerned. That is, until... she rolls to her back and smiles up at me.

"I think I'll share more fantasies," she says with a sparkle in her blue eyes.

"I'll do my best to make them come true."

SOPHIE

"*Y*ou're off to a good start."

"Sophie, was it too—?"

"Matt, that was...I don't have words. How could you possibly know my fantasy?"

Matt grins as he falls to my side and pulls me against his chest. "You're okay? I didn't hurt you, did I? I never want to hurt you."

My palm covers his cheek, and I rub the scruff that felt so good at my core. "I'm serious, how did you know? I mean, I didn't know if that was really possible. It was like every book but a million times better."

"Sophie, you're my fantasy too. I've never been like that. You make me lose control. I want to do things to you that I've never done before." His expression saddens, "But I don't want to scare you away. If it's too much—"

"How can you scare me away? I'm yours forever."

Matt sits up and looks down at me. Slowly and gently,

he tugs my hair until it's fanned over the pillow. "You're more beautiful than I remember, more stunning than your pictures." He touches my lips. "You're also the sunshine I remember. Your smile is addicting and contagious. I love seeing your lips all pink and bruised. I think I'll keep them like that forever."

"Forever?" I ask.

"Is there anything stopping your forever? I'll marry you tomorrow, or is it today?"

"I start college in two weeks."

"I can afford whatever you want. You don't need to go to school. I know your major. My company has lots of events. You can work for me, for us," he corrects. "Marry me, and it will be half yours."

I shrug. "I think I want all of it—marriage and education. Is that too much?"

He leans down and kisses my nose. "If that's what you want, then that's what we can do."

I swallow, thinking about my grandparents. "Can we take this slow? Like maybe not get married—"

I stop speaking as his eyes narrow.

"Listen," I say hurriedly. "Not get married *tomorrow* or today," I add with a smile. "I know you've been married before, but I haven't. I'd like a wedding. How about after my first semester?"

His body stiffens. "None of that dorm shit. You're living with me. There's no way I'm leaving you alone with college boys."

"Why would I want a boy when I have a man?"

His chest rises and falls. "I trust you. It's them I don't trust."

"My grandparents..."

Matt takes a deep breath. "Okay. We can ease them into it. Is your first semester paid?"

I nod.

"Including housing?"

"Yes...*Sir*," I add with a grin.

Matt shakes his head. "Be careful. I'm ready to take you again."

"Real life or fantasy?"

His lips connect with mine. When he finally pulls away, I'm lost in the emotion of his green eyes. It's like I'm all he can see. "Sophie, whatever you need to have— real life or fantasy—I'll never deny you. I'm the man to give you what you want."

"Yes, you are, but only forever. How about I start at the dorm, but" —I shrug my shoulder— "I spend whatever time here you want me to spend?"

"That's every minute of every day. It'll be hard for you to get to class."

"One day at a time."

"As long as one thing is clear: you're mine." Matt reaches down and cups my core. "And this pussy is mine. No one, not even you, can bring it pleasure. That's my job." His brow lengthens. "Is that understood?"

"Yes, Sir."

I giggle as he moves on top of me.

"I warned you."

"I guess I'm a slow learner."

"Tell me, Sophie. What other fantasies have you had?"

I look down, but the way he's on top of me, I still can't see his cock. "I still haven't seen you."

"I'm big."

My eyes widen. "I know that."

"You want to see my cock?"

"I do."

"What will you do to see it?"

I swallow, thinking of the books I've read. Before I can speak, Matt rolls off of me, covering himself with the sheets and giving me the answer. "Beg."

"Beg to see your cock?"

He nods and tips his head toward the floor. "On your knees, now."

My pulse races as I crawl from the big bed to the floor. Lowering myself to my knees, I bow my head. "Sir, may I please see your cock?"

My wet thighs grow wetter as I wait for his answer. I keep my head bowed, like scenes I've read. It's his feet I see first, right in front of me. It takes all my self-control not to lift my eyes as his stance widens.

"Because you've been a good girl, I'll not only let you see it, you may also suck it."

I lick my lips in anticipation as I lift my chin.

Fuck!

It's huge.

It's rock-hard and pointed upward. A lump forms in my throat as I imagine that giant thing inside of me.

"Sophie," Matt says softly. "Take a breath. You're all right. You can do it."

"It's so big."

"Like that manatee?" he asks with a hint of laughter to his voice.

"I didn't try to suck the manatee. The manatee wasn't inside me."

His soft laugh grows, rumbling through the bedroom. "No, it wasn't, but I was. You can do this. Remember you wanted to taste my come?"

I nod.

He reaches for my chin. "You can tell me no, or you're tired, or not tonight. I'll always listen."

I try to swallow again. "Sir, I want to try."

His chest rises and falls as he grasps his length. "Have you...?"

With my eyes still too wide, I shake my head.

"Think of it like a popsicle, a warm, really big popsicle."

I smile. "I always liked popsicles."

"Open your mouth, and watch those teeth."

Closing my eyes, I do as he says. Musk fills my nose and touches my tongue as I lick the tip. When I do, his cock twitches. I open my eyes to see Matt's eyes closed. Slowly, I open my lips wider and take a little more inside. It's tart and salty. I bob my head. Inch by inch, I work him, taking him deeper until his length reaches the back of my throat.

Though he started this fantasy all domineering-like, as I have him between my lips, Matt is anything but. He's in a state of bliss, letting me have my way. With each suck and lick, I'm filled with a sense of control. I'm in charge of his pleasure, and it's empowering.

I keep going as his cock grows even harder. Adding my hands, I fist what won't fit in my mouth and roll his balls in my fingertips. His breathing quickens and stance widens.

"Sophie, I'm..." He tries to push me away, but I reach for his legs. I know what's coming, and I want to taste every drop.

It's as he comes that Matt reaches for my head and gently thrusts into my mouth. Hurriedly, I swallow, gulp after gulp. It's not like anything I've ever tasted. Once he's done, I continue to suck and lick. His legs grow slack in my grasp as I keep working, making sure I've cleaned every drop.

"Fuck, Sophie. That can't be your first blow job."

I stand, reaching my tiptoes, and kiss him deeply. He wanted me to taste myself. I want the same for him. As our kiss ends, I say, "It was. I'll try to work on my technique. Tell me what I need to do."

Shaking his head, Matt says, "Move in tonight because you're a natural."

SOPHIE

I flop down on the bed in my dorm room. My roommate, McKenzie, seems nice enough, but she's not who I plan on spending most of my nights with. After our first few days of classes, I'm more than ready to spend time at Matt's place.

Though Matt wasn't sure about me living in the dorm, living here makes it a lot easier to slip away than from my grandparents' house. I was never able to spend a full night away unless I told them I was at a friend's house. They may be old, but they aren't senile. It didn't make sense that I went from never sleeping over at anyone's house to suddenly being gone every night.

I had lots of girls I got along with in high school but not since Becky had I ever had a best friend. Cindy is probably the closest but more than likely because we work together. Up until Matt, I was too busy to do high-school-girl things. Now, I'm no longer in high school, and with him, I'm no longer a girl. I'm a woman.

Maybe the dorm will help me have that best friend again.

My phone vibrates with a text message:

Matt:

I'LL BE THERE IN FIFTEEN MINUTES.

Me:

DOES THAT MEAN I'LL COME IN SIXTEEN?

Matt:

WEAR A DRESS AND YOU'LL COME IN FIFTEEN AND TWO SECONDS.

Me:

CONFIDENT MUCH?

Matt:

DO YOU DOUBT ME?

Hell, no, I don't doubt him. I'm already wet, and he's not even near me.

Me:

NO, SIR. NEVER.

Matt:

FUCK. I'M RUNNING STOPLIGHTS. I'LL BE THERE IN TEN.

Me:

DON'T GET PULLED OVER. I'LL HAVE TO TAKE

MATTERS IN MY OWN HANDS.

Matt:

DON'T EVEN JOKE, BEAUTIFUL. I'LL PUNISH YOUR ASS. YOUR PUSSY IS MINE.

Me:

LOVE YOU.

Matt:

I LOVE YOU TOO. I'M READY TO SHOW YOU HOW MUCH.

I can't stop the goofy smile. It's only been four weeks, but it's been the best four weeks of my life. And now we'll be able to spend more time together.

It isn't like Matt's always available either. He has work. He has other obligations. But when we are together, it seems like it's only us. No one else matters.

"Hey, Sophie," McKenzie says as she opens the door and comes in our room, throwing her backpack on her bed. "Ready for dinner?"

"I'm sorry. I'm going to go out with a friend."

Her eyes widen. "A friend or a boyfriend?"

It's hard for me to think of Matt as a boyfriend because he isn't a boy, but then again, that is what he is. I could say fiancé, but I don't have a ring yet. That hasn't stopped him talking about the wedding.

I'm trying to decide if I want one in town or a destination wedding. With starting university and moving out of my grandparents' house, it's all been so much. The idea of getting married has me excited but also exhausted. It seems like lately all I want to do is sleep. That's why I haven't seen Matt for a few days.

Now, I'm beyond ready.

I shrug. "Boyfriend, but he's not a boy."

She jumps to the end of my bed and sits with a pounce. The movement makes me bounce and giggle.

"Tell me!" she says. "So...is he older?"

"Yes."

"Have you guys done it?"

My cheeks grow hot. "Yes. Have you?"

Is this what college is about, having girl talks with your roommate?

I'm not sure, but in a way, I like it. Since Matt and I have been seeing one another, he's convinced me to take a step back from the Ritz and concentrate on school. That isn't completely true. He wants me to concentrate on him but school also because it's what I want.

McKenzie nods. "Yeah, Justin and I've been together for over a year. He'll be here this weekend. He goes to Florida State. We figure we'll switch off weekends." Her nose scrunches. "Sorry, I know I should have asked. I'm just glad you have a boyfriend too. Where does he go?"

"He doesn't. He's out of school."

"Oh! Like graduated?"

"Yeah," I say, not telling her that he's not only graduated undergrad, but postgrad, like ten years ago. Truth is, Matt is thirty-six.

"I can't wait to meet him."

I stand, straightening the skirt of my sundress, and reach for my purse. "One day. And hey, the weekend thing is cool with me. I probably won't be here a lot. The guy I'm dating has a house off campus." A multimillion-dollar home on the water, but saying that seems like overkill.

Suddenly, the door to our dorm room opens, and a girl about our age peeks her head in. "Sorry," she says. "I'm not trying to bother you, but someone told me that Sophie Hawkins is here."

I narrow my eyes. There's something about this girl that's familiar. It's her eyes, her green eyes. "I-I'm Sophie."

Our door flies open, and the green-eyed girl rushes toward me, wrapping me in a hug. "Oh my God, it is you! I'm Becky! Becky Hamilton! Do you remember me?"

My eyes open wide. "Becky! It's been forever!" And I'm going to marry your dad.

Yep, this didn't seem like the right place to say that.

"Oh my gosh! Sophie, I'm so sorry we haven't kept up." She turns toward McKenzie. "Hi, I'm Becky Hamilton. Sorry to bother you two, but I just had to see if my best friend *ever* is really in my dorm."

"Your dorm?" I ask. "You live here too?" *Why didn't Matt tell me?*

"Yes, just three doors down. Let's catch up. We can order pizza. You still like pizza, don't you?"

I nod. "I do, but—"

"But Sophie can't," McKenzie volunteers. "She's got a hot date with an older guy."

My stomach twists at my roommate's honesty. If only she knew.

"Really? Cool!" Becky says.

My phone buzzes.

Matt:
WHERE ARE YOU?

I try to force a grin. "I do, and he's here." I give Becky a quick squeeze. "Maybe another day?"

"Okay. Hey, have fun!"

I just nod again as I hurry out of my room and toward the front of the building.

MATT

*M*y dick doubles in size just seeing Sophie walk from the glass doors to the car. It's a new Audi convertible. I just bought it today.

It takes her a second to spot me. I know she is looking for my usual Jaguar.

Her smile grows as I jump out and open the passenger door for her.

"Nice dress," I whisper close to her neck. Just before closing the door, I add, "That better be all you're wearing."

She doesn't answer, but by the way her cheeks fill with pink, I know my good girl has followed my instructions.

Once I'm back in the driver's seat, I lean over and give her a kiss. Damn, she tastes so good. My tongue probes her lips, sliding past the flavored gloss and into her sweet mouth.

"Nice car," she says after our kiss ends.

"Do you like it?"

"I do."

I put the convertible in gear, and we make our way toward the campus's main drag. "Good, I debated on the color."

She scans the silver hood. "It's classy. I like it."

I reach into the cup holder and pull out a key fob. Handing it to her, I say, "That's good because it's yours."

The color drains from her face. "What? No. I can't."

"You're the woman I love and will soon be Mrs. Matthew Hamilton. My wife can't be taking the bus and Ubers."

"But it's too much. I can't pay you back."

I let my hand reach for her thigh. "You don't have to. All you have to do is be you. That makes me happy." My fingers grip tighter.

"Matt?" Her head turns from side to side. "This is, umm, open. People can see."

She's right, it is open. The top is down and so are the windows. I watch as her long hair blows around her face. She's a vision.

"I believe that I promised you something," I say as my hand moves higher. "As it is, I'm already beyond my time schedule."

"Matt..."

"Lift that skirt, Sophie, let me see that pretty blonde pussy."

Her shiny lip disappears behind her teeth as she

slowly lifts the skirt of her sundress. Inch by inch she exposes her tanned, fit thighs.

"Spread those legs. I want to see your come, the way it shines in the sunlight."

Through the top of her dress, her nipples harden, tenting the material. "Beautiful, tell me there's no bra under there."

"I'm not wearing a bra," she whispers.

"Fuck, keep lifting that dress."

Her breathing quickens as we enter the freeway. "Matt?"

The bucket seats are low. That doesn't mean that some trucker or maybe even a horny mom in a minivan can't see down, but they can't unless they're looking. I don't plan to let her be exposed that long, but fuck, I need to see her.

"Sophie." My tone isn't asking.

I suck in a breath as she bunches her dress near her waist. On the soft leather is her bare ass. Her neatly trimmed blonde bush is barely visible. It's the glistening come on her thighs that has my attention.

"I need to taste you."

She turns toward me, waiting. When she said her fantasy was a man to teach her and show her, it's become my life's mission. I adore the way she listens and obeys. "Finger yourself and let me taste you."

"Oh, Matt."

"Now."

Her fingers spread her folds as one disappears

inside her.

"How does it feel?"

"Good, but not as good as when you do it."

"That's it. Now add another. Your pussy is used to my cock. One of your little fingers isn't going to do it." Her tits heave as she adds another finger. "Get them nice and wet." My cock grows even harder as I remember to watch the traffic. "Now let me suck them."

Fucking nectar.

I taunt her finger with my tongue, sucking and licking. By the time I'm done, her head is against the seat, and even with her sunglasses on, I can tell her eyes are closed.

"Tell me what you're thinking."

"I'm thinking that if you don't fuck me soon, I may combust."

I laugh. "I thought we were going to dinner."

She shakes her head. "Pizza delivery at your house."

"Is that an order?"

"Yes, Sir, it is."

I reach over and pull down her dress. "We're getting off the freeway." I look into her blue eyes. "That pretty pink pussy is only for me. We're not showing it to the neighbors."

As soon as I pull into the garage, I release my seatbelt. The garage door is closing as I walk around and open her door. I reach for Sophie's hand, helping her from the car. *Help* is a nice way to say that I pull her into my arms and slam the door.

Spinning her back toward the car, I whisper, my voice rumbling menacingly near her ear. "Do as you're told. Hold on to that door because I'm taking you right here, right now."

"Fuck yes."

"Yes?"

Her breathing is labored. "Yes, Sir." Her small hands grip the top of the door as I use my knee to spread her legs. In a quick ninja move, my belt is undone, fly unzipped, and boxers pushed low.

With my dick in my hand, I line it up with her perfect pussy. No buildup. No foreplay—unless the car counts. And I slam into her.

"Oh, Matt!"

Balls deep, I fill her completely, over and over. It isn't until I notice her blanching fingers that I even register the sound of us coming together. She's so fucking wet; it's like a tiny slip-and-slide tunnel squeezing my cock. Each thrust is bliss.

In the few weeks Sophie and I've been together, I love the way she's opened up. There's nothing shy about her, the way she loves making love. She's the most responsive woman I've ever known.

"God, Matt, don't stop."

I have no plans to stop, ever.

"Harder!"

Pulling her ass higher, I do as she says, harder and faster, my body pounding against her ass until we both explode. It is a fucking free fall from a thousand feet up as we float back to earth.

I lean down, still connected, and kiss her neck. "Hi, sweetness, I've missed you. How were your last few days of college?"

She cranes her neck toward me. Even in the dimly lit garage, I can see the sparkle in her blue eyes. "I thought they were good. But nothing compares to this." She stretches her neck to kiss me. "I've missed you too."

"Me or my cock?"

"Both."

I move in and out of her. It's like I'm perpetually hard in her presence. Even a cataclysmic orgasm doesn't take away my erection. "How about slow this time?"

Her head drops forward. "Only if you make me come like that again."

"Challenge accepted."

SOPHIE

Wearing only Matt's shirt, I cuddle next to him on the couch. Some football game is playing on his giant TV as I nibble a slice of pizza. It seems like I'm always hungry, but when I eat, my stomach gets all upset.

He looks at me with concern in his green eyes. "Sophie, you need to eat more." His grin returns. "I know I've already used up more than one slice of pizza's strength, and I'm not letting you leave until I fuck you at least two more times."

I shake my head. "I thought old men couldn't get it up."

Matt reaches for the plate and sets it on the floor as his body covers mine. He's changed from his early suit pants into jeans. The way they hang low on his hips should be illegal, especially when he's not wearing a shirt.

"Oh, you're going to regret that," he warns. "I don't

think I'm returning you to your dorm until tomorrow morning. You'll find out just how long I can stay up."

I giggle as he leans forward and sucks my nipple.

"I swear that all this attention is making your tits bigger."

I laugh. "Are you saying they're too small?"

He leans back and his eyes narrow. "Sophie, when was your last period? I don't remember you ever having one."

My chin drops to my chest. I knew this was coming, I just didn't know how to be the one to bring it up.

Matt lifts my chin. His green eyes are now wide with wonder and a sense of expectancy. "Have you had one? Since...us?"

I shake my head and quickly shrug. "You said you wanted a baby."

He jumps off me, off the couch. It's comical because his jeans are unzipped and the tip of his cock is peeking over his boxers. Yet for the first time, he's not thinking about sex. He's grinning from ear to ear. "Are you sure?"

Though I nod, I say, "I haven't taken a test, but I'm late, really late. Like two weeks. From what I read, you probably got your wish. It probably happened our first night."

He reaches for my hands and pulls me off the couch. "Sophie, I don't say it enough. I love you." His hand goes to my stomach. "And I already love our baby. We need to celebrate. This is the best news ever."

All of a sudden, Matt pulls me through the open glass doors onto the pool deck.

"Matt, I'm" —I look down at his half-buttoned shirt I'm wearing— "not dressed."

"This is where it all started." He gestures around the pool deck. "This is where I want to marry you. Here, at our house. We'll go tomorrow and buy you the wedding dress of your dreams, and then to the jewelry store for the biggest ring. Lastly, we'll go talk to your grandparents." His brows knit together. "I know they'll probably hate me at first, but I'll swear on my life to be the best husband to their granddaughter and best father to their great-grandchild."

"We talked about waiting."

"That was when it was just us. Now it's" —he motions between us— "us."

"Maybe I should take a test."

"Oh, I need to call Becky!"

Her name brings back my shock at seeing her. My steps stutter as I fall into one of the cushioned chairs still wearing only his shirt. "You know we used to be best friends?"

Matt sits beside me. "Why do you look sad? You can be again. I'm sure she'll be thrilled to see you."

"Does she know...about us?"

He tilts his head. "She knows I'm seeing someone."

"She does? You talk?"

"Of course we talk. Sophie, I love being a dad. I love my daughter. I'll love all my children." He squeezes my hand. "All of them. Sophie, we're going to be parents!"

I sigh. I think there was a part of me that was

worried about his and Becky's relationship. If they weren't close, what did that mean for our children? "I need to tell you something."

"Anything."

"I saw her—Becky. She found me. Tonight, right before you picked me up."

Matt's eyes close. "Fuck, I'm so overwhelmed with you that I never thought about you two at the same college."

"So you knew she was there?"

"Of course I did. I mean, I'm paying the bill. I didn't help her move in only because her mom wanted to. We agree to coexist."

"How do you think she'll feel about being a big sister?"

"She already is," Matt says. "Her mom has other kids. Becky is great with them."

"It was so good to see her. I've missed her, but I'm afraid she's going to hate me."

"Never. Once best friends, always best friends."

I scrunch my nose. "And you don't think it's a little weird that I'm having my best friend's father's baby?"

Holy cow! The reality hits me. I'm having my best friend's dad's baby!

Matt laughs. "You're having *my* baby. The rest is just bonus."

I shake my head. "She lives three doors down from me."

Matt scans the pool deck and beyond. "Unless you're

saying she lives in that house over there, then you're wrong."

"At the dorm."

"Sophia Hawkins, soon to be Hamilton, my baby is not living on dorm food or resting on some bed that eight years' worth of freshmen have slept and screwed on."

"But..."

"But what? Now you have a car. You can drive to classes."

I shake my head. "I can't cook."

Matt's smile grows. "That's okay. I have a cook."

I look around. "You do? I've never seen her."

"She doesn't live here. And she also knows about you. She's giving us our privacy."

"But...what about my clothes?"

"We'll move your stuff here as soon as possible."

"I can't go to class tomorrow in the same sundress."

Matt reaches for my hand and pulls me into the house. "Come with me."

As we go up the stairs, I ask, "Is this my lesson on your ability to stay erect?"

He peers over his broad shoulder with a grin. "No, but it could be."

Entering his room, he bypasses the bed and leads me toward his closet. I've been in there before. Like everything else in this house, it's big. This time, my steps stop at the entry. One side is filled with women's clothes.

Dresses, slacks, jeans, and tops. There's a rack filled with all different styles of shoes.

I reach for a shoe. It's my size.

I pull a dress from the hanger. It's my size.

"How?"

"I'm a man of many talents."

"Matt?"

"Okay. It wasn't me. I hired a personal shopper." His green eyes shine. "She can buy your maternity clothes too, or you can. The particulars are up to you."

I look down at my stomach. With only few of the buttons on his shirt closed, I can see my tanned skin and my hip bones. "Pregnant."

I sink to the soft carpet.

Matt follows after me, landing on his knees.

MATT

$\mathcal{O}$h no. Is she sick? Sophie's cheeks are pale and so are her lips. "Sophie, are you all right? What's the matter?"

"Matt, I'm pregnant."

My cheeks rise. "Yes, we've established that. Do you want to get a test to be sure?"

"I'm going to get fat. Will you still like me when I'm fat?"

"No."

Her blue eyes widen and immediately fill with tears.

I pull her close. "Stop. I won't *like* you...well, I will. I will *love* you. I do, forever and always." I stroke her long hair. "I think I always have. From the first time I saw you, I knew you were sunshine. You still are, Sophie. That's what you bring to my life.

"I live in the Sunshine State and somehow the sun forgot to shine on me. Until you. In the short time we've been together, my whole world has changed. As soon as I open my eyes in the morning, I think of you. I can't wait to finish my latest business deal so I can be with you.

"You've given me a purpose to breathe." I touch her stomach, splaying my fingers over her warm skin. "And the night you gave me the honor of your most prized possession we made a baby. It's a miracle and so are you. There is nothing I won't do for you because you have done everything for me."

My speech is real and from the heart. It was supposed to make her happy, but instead, more tears fall from her closed eyes and down her cheeks.

I push her to arm's length and stare. "Open your eyes." She immediately obeys. The lifting of her lids is like opening a floodgate, allowing more tears to fall. "Is this wrong? Do you not want me?"

She lifts the tails of my shirt that she's wearing, exposing her sensual body, and wipes her eyes. "I can't believe you've made all my fantasies real. When my parents died, I thought I'd never have a real family again. You've given me everything I've ever dreamed of. I don't only love you, but I want you."

I narrow my gaze. "You *want* me?"

She nods, once again tucking her lip behind her teeth.

Reaching down to my unbuttoned jeans, I fist my cock. Its width grows at my own touch. "How about this? Do you want my dick? Does your pussy want it?"

Her lip breaks free. "So fucking bad. I'm not experienced enough to know, but I think it's the hormones. Every second I'm awake, I need to have you inside me."

I look over her shoulder. "Our bed is right over there."

"Ours?"

"Yes, ours."

She shakes her head. "It is, but I need you right now, right here. Slow and gentle. Let's show our baby that Mommy and Daddy love one another even on the closet floor."

I push my jeans and boxers down as she lies back and spreads her legs. The tip of my cock slips through her warm come as it delves deep in her core. "Your wish is my command."

Two days later, I'm reading my tablet next to the pool as Sophie sleeps under an umbrella. She's so adorable. Though I know it's our baby making her tired, I've done my part. It's Saturday afternoon, and we've already had sex two times. Three, but once we never really ended.

She is unquenchable, and I love every minute of it.

Her fantasies have also taken on a more domineering tone. Last night, when she asked me to tie her hands, I remembered Dr. Kizer's words about trust. Even in this short time, Sophie trusts me with her love, body, and fantasies. I have no doubt that she is my every dream, fantasy, and life.

Before our little bondage session, we had dinner with her grandparents. It started as I predicted. They were shocked at my age and weren't happy—with either of us.

But I told them what I've told Sophie. I love her. I have loved and will love her forever, and more than life itself, I need to have her. I will spend the rest of my life making sure she's happy.

If that means she finishes college while married and a mother, then so be it. If it means after this semester, she'll take me up on the offer to quit school and go straight to running the events of our company, that is fine too. If she decides to stay home and pop out a million babies, that is also fine. My goal is to make her fantasies come true—no matter what they include.

I'm not convinced that her grandparents believe me, but I understand. Actions speak louder than words. Right now, my action is moving her into our home. In two weeks, we're taking the weekend and going to Key West. I'd said we'd be married here at the house, but Sophie wanted something else. I was willing to go to someplace more exotic, but Sophie is afraid for her grandparents to travel that far.

In two weeks, the stunning sleeping woman under the umbrella will be Sophie Hamilton. We only have one more person to invite.

I pick up my phone and open my recent calls. Taking a deep breath, I hit *CALL*.

"Hey, Beck. It's Dad."

"Hi."

"Do you have time for lunch with your old man tomorrow?"

"Gosh, I don't know. I could probably pencil you in." Her laughter makes me smile. "Guess who I saw?"

"Who?" I ask, knowing her answer.

"You'll never believe it. I don't know if you remember her but Sophie Hawkins. She was my best friend when we were younger."

I take a deep breath and look over at Sophie. "I remember."

"She's here. Well, I haven't seen her for the last few days, but she lives right down the hall from me."

Not anymore, but I didn't say that.

"Best friends are hard to come by," I say. Yes, I know I sound like a dad. "I bet she was happy to see you."

Becky laughs. "I think so. She was taking off on a date with some hot dude."

Hot dude?

"Remember that I told you that I started seeing someone?"

"Yeah."

"And you're okay with that?" I ask, knowing her answer won't change the way I feel about Sophie.

"Of course, Dad. Even old guys should be happy."

"Hey, thanks. I wondered if you'd like to meet her tomorrow."

"Well, shit. Now our lunch plans are in ink. I want to meet the first woman you've been serious about since Mom."

"Okay. How about here at the house? Do you want me to pick you up?"

"No. I can drive," she says. "I love my new car. It was the best graduation gift ever."

"You know that just because I found someone doesn't mean I love you less."

"Stop being all mushy. Someday I'll meet someone too. Actually, I may have, and you'll always be my dad."

She met someone?

"Love you, Beck. See you tomorrow. Noon?"

"I should be awake by then."

MATT

Waking Sunday morning, I stare in awe at the beautiful woman beside me. Her long golden hair lies upon her pillow, her lips are pink and parted, and her long lashes flutter with REM sleep. Lifting my head to my fist, my elbow on the bed, I continue to take her in. The sheets are twisted around her shapely legs, leaving her midsection and above exposed.

The woman in my bed is stunning.

No makeup and mussed hair.

I resist the urge to wake her.

The way my dick aches and stands to attention below the sheet, I don't know how long I will be able to resist touching and waking her. Hell, she was the one to wake me sometime during the night for another round of sex.

I've never been so perpetually hard.

My dick is acting like I'm the eighteen-year-old.

The reality of our age difference registers in a way it hadn't before.

Today we're going to tell Becky that her childhood best friend will soon be her step-mother and that in eight months, she'll be a big sister again. Beck's mother has two young children with her new husband.

I'd been as young as Sophie when Beck was born. Life back then had been more difficult, emotionally and financially. I would like to think I've been a good dad, and despite the issues in my first marriage, her mother and I gave Becky a sense of security.

As I watch Sophie sleep, I'm grateful for another chance. I won't love this new baby any more than I do Becky, but damn, I'm excited to be the husband Sophie needs and father to our child.

Sophie's eyelids flutter as the gorgeous blue of her orbs comes into view. The tips of her lips curl upward before she speaks.

"Are you watching me sleep?" she asks.

The sound of her voice makes me smile. "Yes, and you're beautiful."

She turns toward me. "I don't know if that's creepy or sweet."

Lowering my head, I brush my lips over hers. When our gazes again meet, I say, "Whatever you want it to be."

"Hmm," she hums. "More of my fantasies."

"I have one," I admit, trusting her as she's trusted me. "You do?"

"Do you want to hear it?"

Her pink lip disappears behind her front teeth. "Um, yes." Her petite hand comes to my cheek. "I want us to be completely open with one another. I trust you and even the other day when you tied my hands, I knew I would be safe and loved. What do you want me to do?"

I reach for her hand and kiss her palm, before lowering it under the sheets. My eyes close as she fists my hard dick. With simply her touch, my balls retract. Damn. "I want *you* to fuck *me*. Ride me." I turn to see her smiling face. "I want to watch you."

She takes a deep breath. "On top? Me?"

"Unless, you don't—"

She wiggles from the twisted sheet, her perfect nude body on display as she pushes my chest back and climbs over me. From my vantage, her luscious tits are right before my eyes as she positions herself over my torso. I strain my neck to catch one of her nipples, and I suck.

Sophie's back straightens as she pulls away. "No, Sir," she says with a grin. "You want me to fuck you. I'm the one in charge."

I can't hold back my smile. "It's an illusion that at this moment, I'm enjoying."

"Good." She lifts her tight ass as her hands hold onto my shoulders. "Now, no touching. Put your hands behind your head."

Doing as she says, I reply, "You are cute when you think you're in charge."

Her blue eyes disappear as she positions the tip of my dick at her entrance. Her grip disappears as she works herself, sheathing my length in small increments. It takes all of my willpower not to buck upward or tug her down. Inch by inch, her fucking tight, warm pussy stretches, taking me in. I watch as her face contorts, morphing from thought to ecstasy.

"Oh," she moans as her body quivers.

"That's it, Sophie, take me all the way."

"God, Matt, I'm so full like this."

My hands itch to move, to grab ahold of her hips and pull her in place. "I need you to move, or I'm going to do it."

Her grin returns as she shakes her head. "No, remember? Your fantasy." Leaning back down, her fingernails grip my shoulders as slowly, she begins to flex her legs, lifting and lowering herself. Her long hair creates a veil around our faces. Within the golden tunnel, all I can see is her beautiful face. Her pace is painstakingly slow, both erotic and agonizing.

Up and down.

After a bit, her breathing quickens as she speeds up her movements.

I can't take it anymore. Reaching for her hips, I flip us so I'm on top while keeping us connected.

"Matt," she shrieks.

"You're killing me."

"I don't want to do that," she says with a giggle.

I smooth strands of her long hair away from her face. "Good, because I'm going to speed things up a bit."

Sophie nods. "Yes, Sir." Her back arches as I drive

into her. The friction is intense as I reach for her hands, hold them over her head, and suck one nipple and then the other. I'm lost in a fog as I continue kissing, nipping, and sucking. No part of her skin is safe as I nip the sensitive flesh of her neck, collarbone, and lower. My morning scruff leaves her skin pink in the wake of my attention.

She wraps her toned legs around me as I slam her into the soft mattress. Her pussy quivers around my cock seconds before she comes. Our bedroom fills with her whimpers and moans before her arms and legs fall slack.

"I'm not done," I say, pulling out and moving my beautiful fiancée to her hands and knees. Craning her neck over her shoulder, her blue eyes gleam. "Are you ready for more?" I ask as I tease her wet cunt with my fingers.

"Yes." Her answer is more than words as she responds, her pussy tightening around my fingers.

In no time, I'm again balls deep, pounding into her warm haven from behind. My fingers blanch as I hold tightly to her hips until I feel the burn building within me. My muscles strain as I prod harder and harder. She's calling out my name as she comes again.

All at once the wave hits me, and I let out a primal roar. My dick throbs as I come, filling her to overflowing with my seed.

When I pull out, I roll onto my back and bring Sophie with me. Our breathing slows to normal as our hearts beat as one. Stomach to stomach, her tits flatten against the hardness of my chest. I lift her face and kiss her pink lips. "You're amazing."

Her head shakes. "I think that was you. Remember, I was apparently killing you."

"I definitely like you on top, but damn, my patience was expiring fast."

"I liked it, but..." her words trail away.

"But what?"

"I'm sorry." Her gaze meets mine. "I'm sorry I'm so inexperienced. You probably want—"

My finger comes to her lips. "I want you, Sophie. You are just the right amount of experienced for me."

"Is it bad that I like you to be in control?"

"No, that's not bad. I like that too. I also want you to know that it's okay to try new things. I want you to feel like we can tell each other everything."

She shrugs. "I like the way it felt. Maybe I need practice."

"We have time for that." My eyebrows rise. "Now?"

Her grin is back. "I think I need to use the bathroom first."

When she starts to move, I reach for her wrist, stopping her. "Sophie, I wanted to tell you. I invited someone to lunch today."

"Um, okay." She turns toward the clock on the dresser. "It's only nine. Do you want me to leave?"

"Hell no. This is your home too."

"Who did you invite?"

"Becky."

SOPHIE

My stomach drops as I stare into Matt's eyes. "Becky?"

"Yes, Sophie, my daughter and your friend."

"Why didn't you tell me before now?"

His palm comes to my cheek, gently cupping. "Because I was afraid you'd react as you are right now."

"I-I'm not reacting."

"You are. Your cheeks just went pale, and the gleam in your lovely eyes has dimmed."

I reach for the sheet and pull it over my breasts, unsure of what I am thinking or feeling. "I'm pregnant, remember?"

Matt's eyes open wide. "Oh damn, I forgot."

I playfully slap his arm. "I saw Becky the other day for the first time in years, and now she's going to find out about us."

He nods.

"And you think that's okay?" I ask.

"Do you think it would be better just to invite her to the wedding and let her learn there?"

I don't know what I'm thinking. "She'll hate me."

"Why would she hate you, Sophie? At one time you were best friends. You can be like that again."

I shake my head as bile bubbles in my stomach. The nausea is caused by more than the news about Becky. Pushing off from the bed, I run to the attached bathroom and kneel before the toilet just in time. Matt's voice chases after me, but all I hear are my mostly dry heaves. When the uproar of my queasiness finally stops, Matt is beside me, a cup of water in one hand and a dampened washcloth in the other.

"Sophie, I'm sorry. I didn't realize it would upset you this much. I can reschedule and talk to Beck alone."

Standing, I take what he is offering and rinse the bad taste from my mouth. "No, I don't think I got sick because of Becky." My head tilts. "I think it's our baby. I haven't had much sickness, but...I don't know."

He reaches for my hands. "What kind of father do you think I'll be to our baby?"

Images of Matt holding a small baby and playing with a toddler come to my mind as my cheeks raise in a smile. "Amazing. I know you will be. I remember how you were with Becky when we were younger."

"I want to be. What kind of father would I be to Becky if I didn't try to include her in our lives?"

I take a deep breath. "You're right but...I'm scared."

"Of what?"

"That this will end." I motion between us. "Maybe this is a dream and telling Becky will make it end. I'll wake up and..." Tears come to my eyes. "I don't want you to have to choose between Becky and me."

"I'm not."

"What if you have to?"

He wraps his arms around me and pulls me close against his wide chest. Beneath my ear, his heart is pounding out a rhythm. "Can you hear that?" he asks.

I nod. "Your heart? Yes."

"Listen closely."

I do as he says, listening to the *thump, thump*.

"Do you hear what it's saying?"

I look up, my gaze meeting his. "Saying?"

"Yes, Sophie. My heart is saying that it has plenty of room for more people to love."

The tears are back. I think it's the hormones.

He cups my chin and holds my stare. "Wouldn't it be awful if a heart could only love one other person? What would happen when children are born or grandchildren? You love your grandparents, right?"

"I do."

"What about me?"

A smile comes to my lips. "Yes, I love you. It's different."

"Of course it is. That's what my heart is saying. It's possible to love many people. Think about it. What about parents and siblings and good friends?"

I suck in a ragged breath and nod. "Good friends," I repeat. "Do you think Becky and I can be that again?"

"I think she'll be surprised and relieved."

"Relieved?"

"I told her I wanted her to meet the woman I'm dating. She's probably nervous, wondering what that woman is like and if that woman will like her."

I nod. "I guess that would be normal."

"So imagine her excitement when she finds out that the woman I love has loved her too—since they were children."

"You met with my grandparents. I can do this."

He again pulls me close. "How are you feeling?"

"Hungry," I reply with a grin.

MATT

$\mathcal{T}$he doors to the pool deck are open, and a soft, warm breeze skirts around us. Beyond the deck, the water glistens with the midday sun, and high above the sky is a cloudless cobalt shade of blue.

"I can help," I offer as Sophie empties containers of food I picked up at the grocery store into different dishes, placing each on the island in the kitchen.

"You bought it all. That is a help." She shrugs. "One day, I suppose I should learn how to cook."

I take a deep breath and sit on one of the tall barstools near the kitchen island. I don't care if she learns to cook or not. When it comes to Sophie, her cooking isn't what I want to eat.

"Remember," she says, pulling me away from my improper thoughts as she spoons chicken salad into croissants before putting them on a tray, "I'm studying event planning. I learned presentation is equally as important when I worked for a caterer." Her smiling gaze meets mine. "That was before you convinced me to concentrate on school."

"I didn't say that."

Her big blue eyes open wide. "You did too."

"No," I say, standing and moving toward her. "I didn't say *only* school."

"Oh, that's right." She places the tray of sandwiches with the other foods and taps her finger on her pink lips. "Hmm. There was something else I was supposed to concentrate on." She grins. "What was that?"

"Who, not what." I tug her away from the empty containers and into my embrace. Staring down at her, I say the only thing that is on my mind. "Me—concentrate on me."

Her body melts against mine. "You make it hard to think of anything else."

"I love you, and you're absolutely radiant."

She is.

I don't know if it's the pregnancy or just her.

She's wearing a bright yellow sundress, one that the personal shopper picked out. Her hair is mostly pulled back into a low ponytail and her makeup is minimal.

"You're my sunshine, Sophie. I want to keep your beautiful smile shining. That's my job. As for cooking, that's what Kat is for."

"I suppose I'll be meeting her soon, too." She looks down at the spread before us and gathers the containers for the recycling. "This is a lot of food for three people."

I barely let her out of my grasp. "I know what I'm hungry for."

"I hope it's chicken salad or maybe fresh fruit."

"No," I say with a grin. But before I can share that she is my desired entrée, the alarm system dings, indicating the opening of the front door. Sophie hurriedly tosses the containers in the recycling and claps the crumbs from her hands. "Matt, I'm going to go out to the pool for a moment."

I reach for her hand. "Sophie."

"No," she says adamantly, "we aren't ambushing her. Go, greet Becky. Give her a second to understand."

I nod, knowing that Sophie is probably right. I was so confident in this reunion that I didn't consider the possibility, as Sophie said, of ambushing my daughter.

"Dad?" Becky calls from the foyer. "Where are you?"

I wait only a few seconds until Sophie slips through the open doorway to the pool deck. "In the kitchen, Beck," I reply.

A few seconds later my daughter is there, her bright green eyes shining as she looks around the kitchen before giving me a quick hug.

"So there's food." She peers my way. "Where is this mystery woman?"

"Lemonade?" I ask, gesturing toward the pitcher on the counter.

Her head tilts. "Will I need something stronger?"

"You aren't old enough for anything stronger."

She plucks a piece of pineapple from the bowl of

mixed fruit and eats it. "Did you call me over on false pretenses? I'm excited to meet whoever caught your attention." When I don't answer, she asks, "Are you or are you not dating?"

"It's even more than that, Beck."

Her eyebrows lower. "You got married without telling me?"

"You know I wouldn't do that."

"Oh my God, Dad, just tell me. The suspense is killing me."

"How do you feel about me marrying again?"

She shrugs as she sits on a tall stool at the kitchen island with the pool deck behind her. "I'm not a little kid. I guess I want you to be happy."

I let out the breath I was holding. "I am, Beck. I'm in love."

She scrunches her nose. "Please don't go into too much detail."

"I want you to know that I love you too. I always will. And now that I found, or refound, someone, I want us all to be a family." I start to tell her about the baby but stop myself as Sophie appears in the doorway.

Becky nods. "If you want that, why are you hiding her?"

"He isn't. I am," Sophie says.

Beck spins toward her. "Sophie." Beck jumps up. "Oh, what are you doing here?" It's as Becky approaches Sophie that the metaphorical dots begin to connect in her head. "Wait. What *are* you doing here?" Beck turns to me. "Dad?"

Sophie doesn't move from the doorway. Instead, I go to her. "Becky, I'm seeing Sophie."

My daughter's head shakes. "That doesn't even make sense."

I reach for Sophie's hand and squeeze. "I bet it doesn't." I look down at Sophie. "Does it?"

She grins. Her smile brightens the kitchen, the house, the entire world. Her eyes meet mine. "She's right. This makes no sense at all. Sometimes I wonder if it's real."

"Oh, it's real."

"Hello."

Sophie and I turn back to Becky.

"This isn't some kind of joke?" Becky asks.

Sophie and I shake our heads in unison.

"How long has this been going on?" Becky asks.

Letting go of my hand, Sophie walks toward Becky. "About a month. I was afraid to say anything when you came in my dorm room. I guess I'm a bit head over heels."

Becky's nose scrunches. "With *my dad*?"

Sophie nods. "Yes. I love him."

"My dad?"

"Don't you love him?"

Becky looks my way and back to Sophie. "Well, yeah, because he's my dad."

"Beck, I'm sorry," I say. "I didn't expect this to be weird."

"You're dating someone my age, and you thought it wasn't weird?"

"I'm dating a woman who I'm in love with. Age means nothing."

Becky paces around the kitchen island. "Okay, then I think I should let you know that I'm dating someone. He's a professor at the university."

My neck straightened. "One of your professors? That's not right."

Her eyes opened wide. "Age means nothing?"

"Who?" Sophie asks.

"It's not age," I try to reason. "It's his position of authority. There are rules."

"Yeah, I'm not in his class."

"Who?" Sophie asks again.

"Now what do you think?" Becky asks me.

"I want to kick his ass. Do you love him?"

She lets out a long breath. "Do you two—love each other?"

"Yes," we both answer in unison.

Slowly, my daughter approaches Sophie. "I'm not dating anyone or even seeing anyone. I was making a point."

"I can leave if you want to talk to Matt," Sophie offers.

"No," Becky says. "I still think this is all kinds of messed up, but Dad has been alone for a long time. I want him happy." She reaches for Sophie's hand. "Are you...happy?"

"More than I ever thought possible."

Becky takes a deep breath. "Okay." She turns to me. "You said that you're more than dating and less than married. What does that mean?"

"Well," I say, "how about we eat some lunch and chat?"

SOPHIE

The ocean breeze blows strands of my blonde hair around my face as I look up at the most handsome green eyes I've ever known.

Seeing Matt on the beach reminds me of the first time I knew that I loved him. It reminds me of the dreams of a young girl wishing for her prince. As his gaze takes me in, I know that dreams as well as fantasies can come true. From the moment I exited the hotel and walked the path toward him, Matt has only had eyes for me. We are standing on the sand in paradise, yet we could be anywhere because the only thing that matters is the man holding my hand.

"I now pronounce you husband and wife. For the first time," the officiant says, "let me introduce Mr. and Mrs. Matthew Hamilton." He winks at Matt. "It's time to kiss your bride."

"My wife..."

Tears escape my eyes as Matt pulls me close. Our lips unite. I'm expecting chaste, but I've come to understand that Matt undeniably does the unexpected. Instead of brisk, his mouth consumes. My back flexes as he bows me backward, his broad chest smashing my breasts as heat fills my blood and wetness pools between my legs.

"I need to have you, Mrs. Hamilton," he whispers.

My cheeks blush as I stand straight and look out to the chairs. Matthew's parents are here as well as my grandparents. There are also a few friends, but it's the person handing me back my bouquet that means the most to me, well, other than Matt.

"I heard that," Becky whispers with a grin. "Can you two try to keep it under control until you're behind closed doors?"

My cheeks ache from smiling so much. "Talk to your father."

She shakes her head. "No, I like seeing him happy."

I kiss my best friend's cheek. "Me too."

After the reception of food and drinks on a secluded hotel deck overlooking the ocean, we are back in our honeymoon suite.

"Come here, Mrs. Hamilton."

His deep voice sends vibrations to my core that the shimmer in his eyes only accentuates.

"Mrs. Hamilton," I say. "I don't think I'll ever tire of hearing that."

"Good," Matt says, "because you're stuck with it forever."

Our lips meet again. With no concern of an audience, Matt's tongue probes, stealing my breath as well as my words. I can only form moans as he pulls me close.

"You look amazing in that dress..." His words trail away as the gleam in his smirk intensifies.

"I'm sensing a *but*."

His eyebrows arch up and down. "My wife is very intuitive."

"I think I've got you figured out."

"The dress needs to go."

I am ready for this. I admit it was weird to shop with Becky, considering Matt's her dad, but she never let me feel strange. Instead, she was with me every step of the way to buy what he will find under my long dress.

"Then I need some help. It took Becky and Grandma an hour to get me into this. If I try to get out on my own, I may not succeed until tomorrow morning."

Matt takes a step closer and pulls my hips against him. Through the skirts and lingerie, I can feel his erection under his trousers. I no longer wonder what it looks like or how it feels. I know, and I know I love what he does with it as much as I love him.

"Tomorrow," he says, "will not do. I'll tear it off with my teeth before then."

Spinning in his arms, I offer him the buttons along the back. "No teeth, just buttons."

"Fuck! Are there a hundred?"

I laugh. "Look under the buttons on top. There are hidden ones beneath."

He lets out a long breath.

"See, I do have you figured out. If there had been a hundred," I say as he loosens each hidden button, "then the dress would be ruined, and our daughter would never have the chance to wear it."

"Daughter?" he asks. "Isn't it too early to know?"

"Yes, but if this one isn't a girl, we can try again."

The dress gapes as he eases the sleeves from my arms. As I step out, I'm now wearing a nearly sheer white corset and matching lace panties. Matt takes two staggered steps back.

"Fuck. Sophie, I thought you were gorgeous in the dress, but this..."

I step toward him. "This is your wedding gift. It's time you unwrap it."

EPILOGUE

Sophie

Four years later

"*B*ecky, tell Mommy I don't have to wear this," Michael says to his sister, pulling at the bow tie to his small tuxedo.

"But you do, buddy. Please, it's for me."

Michael huffs with his little arms straight before his body relaxes and he wraps those same arms around Becky's neck. "You look really pretty, sis."

"Thanks, so do you."

Tears fill my eyes as I watch my best friend with her littlest brother. Littlest for now. It seems as though the one inside me is another boy, due in only two more months. I run my hand over my large midsection.

"I'm not pretty," Michael protests.

"No, you're not," Becky says with a grin. "You're handsome. Can you go find Dad and tell him it's almost time?"

Michael nods as he runs toward the dressing room door.

Becky's green eyes move to me. "Stop being so emotional. You're going to make me cry."

I try to laugh. "It's just that you're beautiful. I'm so happy you found your special someone and are getting married. You know Matt and I adore Gregg."

"I couldn't let my best friend have all the fun."

We both turn toward the full-length mirror. Becky's dark hair is styled in a sweeping twist and her wedding dress is a designer original. Nothing but the best, Matt insisted. It's hard to believe we're the same young girls who played dolls together.

"Well" —I force a grin— "at least I can say I introduced you to the love of your life." Gregg had been in one of my classes. We were paired for a project, and I knew he'd be perfect for Becky.

"And so can I," she says.

"You did," I confirm. I kiss her cheek. "I should wait outside and let your mom be in here with you."

"You don't have to leave. You're my matron of honor. Mom's good. She'll be back in here after she makes sure the ushers are seating everyone right."

We both laugh. I may be the event planner, but

Becky's mom always has been the one who thrived on organization.

"Are you sure about me standing up with you," I ask. "Look at me. I'm a boat."

"You're not. You're my best friend, my other mom, and having my next little brother. I'd say that makes you pretty special."

I adjust Becky's necklace and notice her boobs. "When are you going to tell your dad?"

Her eyes grow wide. "What?"

"Beck, your dress has been refitted three times and look at your rack. It's peeking out for the whole world to see. Your little brother is going to have a playmate who, if I'm right, will be about three or four months younger."

"Shit, does Dad know?"

I try to hide my grin.

"How?" she asks.

"Well, believe it or not, your dad knows how babies are made, and he also is very familiar with the changes. My boobs are always our first clue."

"Is he...is he mad?"

"Are you kidding? You're his baby girl. He was ready to kill Gregg."

Becky gasps.

"I'm teasing. Well, kind of. He still wants to hear it from you."

Becky reaches for my hand. "I'm so glad we're still best friends."

"Me too."

———

Later that night, after Michael is tucked into bed, I collapse on our bed with a sigh.

"Becky was radiant today," Matt says.

I smile. "She was. I'm so happy for them."

Matt climbs up the mattress and leans against the headboard. "Did you tell her I knew about the baby?"

I lay my head on his chest. "It may have come up."

He rubs my back. "She told me before we walked down the aisle. I think I finally understand the look your grandpa gave me at that dinner years ago."

Smiling up at him, I say, "He loves you."

"Now, but that night he was ready to take me on. And I know he's like ninety, but knowing what I'd done to his precious granddaughter, he may have taken me down."

"So Gregg?"

"He's a good guy. He loves Becky. But I made him the same promise your grandpa did to me."

I sit up. "What did Grandpa say? You never told me."

Matt shrugs. "He said if I ever hurt you, he'll get me, even if it's from the grave."

"My grandpa said that?"

"Yep, and I made Gregg the same promise."

I settle my head again as Matt splays his hand over my huge tummy. "How's our little guy? Do you think he'd mind if Mommy and Daddy had some fun?"

My head moves back and forth. "Aren't you tired?"

Matt pulls the pillow from behind my back and leans over me. "Sophie, I promised your grandpa I loved you and would be the best husband to you." He spreads my legs as he speaks between kisses to my sensitive skin. "I told him that he'd never need to worry. You and I were undeniable, meant to be."

His gaze meets mine.

"Oh." My back arches as he plunges inside me.

When I open my eyes, his adoring green gaze is shining down. "Go ahead, deny it. Deny we were meant for one another."

A smile returns to my lips. "No, Sir. I can't." I lift my palm to his stubbly cheek. "You're my Prince Charming, you always were. Now make me come."

His laugh rumbles from him to me.

"You're insatiable, especially when you're pregnant."

"It's your job to keep me that way."

Matt brushes a kiss over my lips. "Challenge accepted."

"I love you, Matt."

"I love you, too."

Undeniable.

The magic word.

The End

Did you know that Dr. Kizer's advice has helped other characters?

If you enjoyed UNDENIABLE, be sure to check out UNCONVENTIONAL, UNEXPECTED, and UNFORGETTABLE, all stand-alone novellas in the INDULGENCE series.

Learn Dr. Kizer's secret of success while exploring hidden desires!

Turn the page for sneak peeks!

SNEAK PEEK AT UNCONVENTIONAL

Victor

People try to keep their private information secret, but they don't succeed.

She didn't.

She's in the public eye, available to everyone with the flip of a switch. Turn on the TV and there she is—*Erika fucking Ellis*. Her beautiful face, shapely legs, and entire body is there in UHD in everyone's living room, kitchen, or bedroom. Being in the public eye, she should have known better, been more careful. She should have taken precautions.

She didn't.

Her carelessness pisses me off, infuriates me.

Yet without it, where would we be?

She let down her guard and spoke without thinking.

She isn't the only one who has, but she's the one I've been watching. She's the one who matters.

Obtaining bits and pieces of her life story takes time, but as my mind fills with the possibilities for our future, I know the patience will be worth the reward. The process isn't difficult. It's as simple as standing near her in the coffee shop line.

She concentrates on the menu or the screen of her phone, acting as if I'm not there. But I am, taking it all in.

"Name for the order?" the barista asks.

Close enough to smell her sweet perfume, I hang on her every word.

Suddenly her name is not only announced, but written across her cup.

"Telephone number?" the man at the dry cleaners asks.

A room full of customers and she speaks loud enough for the elderly man to hear.

There it is.

Ten digits that open up a wealth of information.

The rest is easy. An internet search, not even one as comprehensive as done by law enforcement, and much of her information is at my fingertips, just like her hard nipples will soon be.

I dig for more.

Her passwords aren't difficult. The name of her first pet. The dog was mentioned in a personal interview posted by her news station: *Get to Know Erika Ellis*.

That's my plan—to know her better than anyone else.

"Ma'am, can you confirm your date of birth?" With a slight change to my voice, I become an account specialist, in need of clarifying her order. "Why, yes, we have this order scheduled for delivery on Tuesday. Will you be available to sign? ...No ...Is there anyone else over the age of eighteen at your residence...?"

Simple questions that in her preoccupied world she answers without thought. Her recklessness is her downfall, and while I appreciate it for the success of my plan, I plan to punish her for it. If I am able to learn her life secrets, so could anyone, someone, even another man. That thought fills me with rage, propelling my blood downward, away from rational thought and straight to my dick. It's painfully hard with the need to take her, mark her, and make her mine. After all, she is— mine. She always has been. I've known it for some time. It's time she accepts it—all of it and all that comes with it.

It's difficult to hide my erection as I patiently plan, day after day, week after week, following, listening, and paying attention. Like in the coffee shop, most of the time she doesn't even notice me. Like the song 'Mr. Cellophane,' it's as if she looks right through me, walks right past me. Doesn't even know I'm there.

She's too busy—too preoccupied—to comprehend that I'm her future, present, and past. Nevertheless, I'm not deterred. I listen to every word, seize every opportunity. I'm paying attention and learning even when she's unaware.

Even those times that she takes for herself, in her apartment, lost in an erotic novel, she doesn't realize I'm watching. She's too lost in the story. At work, she's too busy meeting everyone's demands. Her priorities are skewed, and it's my job to show her the error of her ways.

Then again, there are other times when she smiles and even says a word or two to me. Times that she's close enough to touch, that our skin brushes over one another's. I live for moments such as those, knowing there will be so many more in our future.

There isn't any question in my mind. With every fiber of my body, I know she wants me too. When our eyes meet or as she brushes past me in a crowded diner, I feel her desire. The connection, no matter how small, is like lightning, radiating off of her like heat from the sun, warming the air and stoking my desire.

In one such encounter, we stand face-to-face, and her pink tongue darts to her lips. Her blue eyes disappear as her lids grow heavy with desire. I hear her message loud and clear. I understand what she doesn't allow her words to say. It's her silent acceptance of what will be—what our future holds. Soon, that pink tongue will dance with mine. Soon, it will beg for my attention as she kneels at my feet.

I know her wants and needs. With the same passwords on every account and every device, I've taken my time to insert myself into her private world. I know the books she reads and the videos she watches on her Tumblr account. No wonder she sometimes seems aloof. She has desires and fantasies that have gone unfulfilled, ones she hasn't shared even with her husband.

Her loneliness is about to end. But like everything in our future, the timing is up to me. I'm the only man for the job.

She's a public figure, and it fucking pisses me off to think that she stars in other men's wet dreams. It's part of the game she plays for the station—perceived availability. It boosts the ratings, but it's fiction. Her availability isn't real. She doesn't belong to them, not to any of them.

She's mine, all mine. I'll be the one who fulfills her desires. I'll be the one to bind and control her. No one else will take my woman to ecstasy. No one else will bring her desires to life—no one but me.

The first day she looked my way and spoke to me—the day our connection forged—I knew we were meant to be together. I've worked my way into her predictable world, and yet she has no idea of my plans, of our future. Her combination of ignorance and arrogance fuels my desire. Erika thinks she has control, she thinks she calls the shots, but just like her appearance of availability on the evening news, her power in our relationship is a delusion, one I've allowed to fester for too long.

I'm a man who needs control. I've allowed her misconception to run its course, but now it's over. My entire body quakes as I imagine the scene: Erika fucking

Ellis on her knees, tears falling from her beautiful eyes as she relinquishes her illusion and embraces our new reality.

Staring through the lens at the screen before me, I watch her tits bounce and her perfect white teeth shine. Her lips are full, glossy, and red as they part with laughter.

How am I supposed to keep this camera steady as her giggles ring through the air? Even with my headset covering my ears, the pitch of her laughter can't be missed. The man in makeup with slicked-back hair beside her is a prick. He doesn't deserve her laughter or her words.

It isn't a real laugh that I'm hearing, I reassure myself. It's part of her act, part of her TV personality. It's simply for the cameras, for the audience. Her real rings of laughter, moans of desire, and screams of pain are for my ears only.

My chest fills with pride to know that I'm the only one to hear those, the only one to love her. Let the chorus begin.

SNEAK PEEK AT UNEXPECTED

Jenn

I bite my lower lip, trying to hold back the tears as I stare down at the papers before me, wondering how it all came down to this. How can six years of marriage be defined and dissolved in a litany of legal phrases, paragraphs, and division of assets?

"You both need to look at the paperwork carefully," Jonas Miller, our attorney, says. "If everything looks good, all you need to do is sign. Once you both sign, for all practical purposes, it's done." His head bobs in agreement. "We need the judge's signature, but basically, it's all done."

All done.

The phrase rings in my head like the clang of bells from an old-time church.

Each ring a memory of happier times gone by.

Taking a sideways glance at my soon-to-be ex-husband, for some reason, my mind goes back to the afternoon he proposed.

Many of my friends tell stories of how they knew the proposal was coming, how they anticipated and planned. Maybe I'm dense, but when Paul popped the question, for me, it was out of the blue. We'd only been dating for six months, meeting for the first time at a work party. He wasn't a coworker at the firm. He was the friend of a colleague and came along at the last minute. That impulsive decision on his part changed our lives—even if we sign today, that change is forever. From the first moment we met, we hit it off. All I can recall from that party was talking to Paul. The rest of the people ceased to exist. Before we parted ways, he entered his phone number into my phone, and unbeknownst to me, sent himself a text.

We were connected.

It wasn't until the next morning when my phone buzzed that I saw the message he'd sent.

From my phone (the text he sent the night before): *"Hey, it was great meeting you. Let's have lunch tomorrow?"*

From his phone the next morning. *"I couldn't respond sooner —I was busy thinking about you. Lunch sounds great. I'll pick you up at noon. Address?"*

I had to giggle. It looked like I'd been the one to ask him

out, but we both knew the truth. He was both sides of the conversation. Of course, I sent him my address along with a smiling emoji.

I hadn't been looking for forever, so when it found me, I didn't recognize it.

Six months later, the two of us went away for the weekend up to a secluded resort in northern Wisconsin. There were no fancy restaurants or tall buildings. Instead, we were surrounded by the beauty of nature. For three days we hiked trails and found remote vistas with stunning views. On the final day, we took off early in the morning, walking until we finally made it to the shore of a quiet, out-of-the-way lake. From his backpack Paul pulled out a blanket, a bottle of Champagne, orange juice, and food. He had all the makings of a picnic breakfast, complete with mimosas. Lying on that blanket, staring up at the fluffy white clouds as they floated across the cobalt-blue sky, we did what had come naturally to us since the night we first met. We talked.

He was unlike the men I'd dated before, strong and assertive yet also attentive and caring.

We shared.

We listened and heard.

As the words on the attorney's papers blur, the heaviness in my heart reminds me that somewhere along the way we lost that essential element of our relationship.

Sometime during the last six years while navigating life's ups and downs, we both lost the ability to listen, or perhaps we lost the desire to make time to listen—to make time for one another.

Talking hasn't been our issue. We speak—sometimes obsessively.

We have both been known to say things we regret.

No, talking isn't our issue.

Listening is.

On that afternoon that seems like a lifetime ago Paul sat up, took my hand, looked into my eyes with his sexy brown-eyed stare, and asked, "Jenn, will you be mine forever?"

As a lump formed in my throat, I found myself lost in his alluring gaze. "Forever?"

"That's a mighty long time…" We both laughed at the reference to lyrics of a song we both enjoyed and could recite in its entirety. He went on. "…but I'm here to tell you—"

"Yes," I said, nodding as I interrupted a classic Prince hit. "It is a long time, and I want to spend it all with you."

"Mrs. Masters," Mr. Miller says, disrupting my thoughts and bringing me back to the present. "Is there a problem with anything in the paperwork?"

"I-I…" I stutter, unable to find the right words. After all we've said and done, I don't know if I can admit that I don't want to sign, that even though I thought I was ready…I'm not. I'm not ready to give up on our forever.

"Jenn?" Paul asks. "We agreed to a no-contest divorce.

Everything is divided equally. If you'd feel better with us each having separate representation...?"

I shake my head.

"Is there something you want that isn't listed?" Paul asks. "If you want to keep the house, you can buy me out. When we talked about it, though, you agreed that it would be a lot for you to maintain alone. The market is good. We should be able to get a decent, if not above-asking, price and then we'll divide the profit down the middle."

"It just seems too final," I finally manage to say as I choke back the emotion, wondering how we got this far.

"It is final," the attorney agrees. "Unless you two need to think about it, but come on... You've both been involved in this marriage. You both agree it's over. You can't expect this to go on forever."

My gaze snaps to our attorney and then immediately to Paul.

Forever.

Forever?

Forever!

As my gaze meets Paul's, more tears sting my eyes, threatening to spill down my cheeks. I search his expression, hoping to see the same emotions I'm feeling. I wish with all my heart he could remember the question he asked me years ago.

I want one more chance.

Silence fills the small conference room.

Loud, thundering silence.

Not even the hum of the air conditioner or the distant tune of the sound system is heard. It's the kind of quiet that echoes in never-ending emptiness.

If this were a movie it would be filled with the ticking of a clock, perhaps punctuated by the shrill scream of an alarm. Then again, even TV shows have learned the power of silence. The lack of the show's familiar tune during the credits following the Red Wedding will forever haunt *Game of Thrones* fans.

It's the unpredictability of silence that embodies the fear of the unknown.

What will follow?

The silence that surrounds us is as powerful as that used for dramatic effects. It hangs heavily in the air, an unmoving fog clouding our future in a cloak of uncertainty.

Finally, Paul reaches out, covering my hand with his own, and stares into my eyes. His warm reassurance is all it takes to disperse the looming cloud.

I swallow, wondering if I've ever been this scared in my life.

I've been frightened for other reasons, but this is different. This isn't about my physical welfare, but about the loss of something I don't know if I can bear to lose.

I'm not scared to be on my own. I can do it. I've been on my own before. I'm scared to lose the one man whom I truly believed was my forever.

Paul's eyes widen, silently questioning me.

With a quick nod of my head, I let him know that I'm listening.

"Dr. Kizer," he says to me, "recommended that trip. She had a travel agent ready who could book everything."

Dr. Kizer has been our counselor, one recommended by a friend. Unfortunately, our result doesn't seem to be the same as the outcome of our friends. They're off to another state and happily married with a little bundle of joy. We're in an attorney's office about to sign divorce papers.

I swallow again, knowing that the reason my mouth is so damp is due to the tears I'm trying not to shed. "I remember, but we said we said we couldn't afford it."

Paul tilts his head toward the papers laid out before both of us. "What if we were wrong?"

"About?" I ask.

"About all of it."

"All of it?" My voice cracks. "From the beginning?"

"No, Jenn. We haven't been wrong since the beginning. What if we're wrong about being able to afford it? What if we can't afford to not try—not to take the trip?

"Two weeks," he goes on. "We call the travel agent Dr. Kizer recommended. We book the trip, and if we're wrong and the marriage is over, when we return home we sign these damn papers." He shrugs his broad shoulders. "If Dr. Kizer is right and we need time alone to really understand one another, then we'll know. No unanswered questions. The worst that can happen is that we spend some of the profit from the house."

"And if she's right and we're not wrong?"

"Then our forever won't be defined in these papers," he says, motioning toward the table.

The edge of my lip quirks upward. "*Forever?*" I ask. "Do you remember that?"

"I do. I remember too much."

I nod my head, knowing what he means. Along with the good memories, we have the bad. Is it worth a two-week delay to maybe get nowhere? "Paul, I'm scared."

"Of what?"

"To have hope."

"It's scarier not to have hope. Don't you think?"

For the first time in months a weight lifts from my chest and my grin blossoms. With only a few words of his, I remember why I fell in love with this man in the first place. "It feels good to smile."

"It feels good to see you smile."

"After making it this far, this change of plans is..." I search for the right word.

"Unexpected," Mr. Miller volunteers.

I stare into my husband's brown eyes. "Yes. An *unexpected* but hopeful detour."

Paul turns toward our attorney. "We're sorry to have wasted your afternoon. My wife and I aren't ready to sign these papers. Not yet."

Mr. Miller's furrowed brow relaxes as his cheeks also rise. "Listen. I'm a divorce attorney. I'm going to be here in two weeks or a month or whenever you need me or if you don't. This line of work can be a bit disheartening, but if I can offer a bit of advice?"

With my hand in Paul's we both nod.

"You mentioned Dr. Kizer?"

"Yes," I say.

"I presume you mean Dr. Ami Kizer, the relationship counselor?"

Again, we both nod.

"That woman has taken some of my best clients away from me. She's one of the good ones." He waves his hand. "Don't worry about me. I'm still charging you for drawing up these papers, but filing them, well, my advice is to take this unexpected chance. If it works, Dr. Kizer has done it to me again. If it doesn't, we're prepared. Either way, you'll know."

Paul and I look to one another.

"Two weeks?" he asks.

My mind fills with deadlines and obligations. "I'm involved in a case...I'm not sure I can get away—"

"You can always sign today and move on," Mr. Miller interrupts, placing his hands on the papers.

"Jenn?"

I nod my head. "Call the travel agent. Let's leave as soon as possible."

SNEAK PEEK AT UNFORGETTABLE

Marji

"The client blushed as she recalled the setting, describing the scene as she entered the cabin. With each implement she recalled, her cheeks grew redder until she finally apologized. I questioned as to whether talking about their encounter made her anxious or embarrassed. With a sly grin toward her husband, the client replied, 'It makes me want to go back.'"

Pulling the earbuds from my ears, I shake my head, pushing the visuals from my mind. With a quick save, using the clients' identification number instead of name, I close out their records and complete the transcription of Dr. Kizer's appointment notes from the day before.

Looking down at the corner of my computer screen, I see that it is nearly seven at night, almost time to leave work and live. That's what is supposed to happen at this time of night. I know that it is because I've read about it in the novels on my Kindle. I've seen the images on television or in movies. I even transcribe a therapist's detailed notes telling me that is the way it should be.

They're all the same.

They're evidence that not everyone lives for work, novels, and Netflix.

The images and stories are of people shedding their work or career responsibilities, and like a butterfly, freeing themselves from their daytime cocoon, the drab outer layer exfoliating and the bright, colorful wings stretching until the butterfly is free and able to take flight.

"Thank you, Dr. Kizer," Mr. Williams says as his wife smiles, her cheeks blushed from whatever discussion has been happening behind Dr. Kizer's closed office door.

The discussion I will be turning into records tomorrow.

That knowledge causes me to straighten my shoulders, not wanting to give away my connection to the clients' intimated details.

As the couple comes to a stop in front of my desk, I can't help but notice the admiration and adoration they share. It radiates off of each of them. There's no hidden anxiety or concern. It's pure, unadulterated trust and esteem, as if they're the only two people in the room. Forget that. They're the only two people now in the world.

Mrs. Williams's head shakes as she tilts her forehead against her husband's shoulder with a soft giggle.

"Um," I say, clearing my throat. "Would you like to schedule your appointment for next week?"

Mr. Williams looks my direction. "Make that two weeks. We're following Dr. Kizer's advice and taking a week away..." He looks down lovingly at his wife. "...just the two of us."

Mrs. Williams nods. "I sent my mom a text and she's going to stay with the kids. I didn't think I was ready for an entire week, but I am."

Please no details.

That's my thought as her cheeks again fill with crimson.

"Then, two weeks," I say, pulling up Dr. Kizer's schedule on my screen. "Two weeks on Thursday at six p.m.?"

"That's perfect," Mr. Williams says as he enters the appointment into his phone. "Oh Marji, do we talk to you about the use of Dr. Kizer's cabin?"

"For next week?" I ask a bit wearily.

"Yes."

I sit taller. "I'm sorry. The cabins are all booked in advance." I hit a few keys on the keyboard, suddenly feeling the same disappointment that is now emanating from the two people before me.

"Dr. Kizer said there was a recent cancellation," Mr. Williams says. "Can you please check?"

"Next week is our anniversary," Mrs. Williams adds with a hopeful grin. "Seven years and it is better than ever." She sighs. "Better than I could have hoped for."

"If this doesn't work out..." Mr. Williams's words to his wife disappear as I type upon the keyboard until the cabin rental schedule appears before me.

To my surprise, there is an opening. "Well, Dr. Kizer was right."

"She always is," Mrs. Williams says, her smile returning bigger than ever as she still holds tightly to her husband's arm.

I don't want to think about what will be happening at the cabin—the scene and the implements: crops, gags, and restraints to name a few. It's really none of my business what two consenting adults choose to do in their spare time. I mean, it's their decision.

I could pretend to be naïve, tell myself that they're going to rent the cabin for a week to hike the trails or picnic near the lake. I could tell myself that it's no different than any other rental, a Vrbo or a time-share.

If I did tell myself any of the above stories, I wouldn't believe me.

Along with scheduling Dr. Kizer's clients, seeing them come in on the verge of marital or relationship collapse and observing their transformations, singularly as well as a couple, as I was doing a few minutes ago, I also transcribe her notes. With an earbud in my ear, I listen to the details as my fingers type, creating a printable record of words of thoughts and feelings that should only be discussed in private.

Of course, what I do is confidential. I wouldn't share a word.

I'm bound to the ethics of my job. That doesn't mean I don't retain the information, sometimes think about it, and sometimes imagine what it would be like to be one of these wives.

Please don't assume I am out to wreck a marriage. That's the farthest thing from the truth. I don't want any of the husbands that come in here for counseling.

No, I want my own.

I'm not even looking for a *husband*, just a man who is capable of indulging in a few fantasies I can't seem to unimagine.

I write the six-digit code on a card and hand it to Mr. Williams. "Here's the code to unlock the cabin. The address is on the back. It's very isolated. There are directions online at the website on the card. Many GPS receivers have difficulty finding it. Please notify the number on the front of the card if you have any specific requests prior to your arrival. Your rental begins on Saturday. Be sure to notify the rental company of those requests by Friday."

"Specific requests?" Mrs. Williams asks. "I was under the impression it's fully...um...furnished...stocked..."

"Yes," I say, working to keep a neutral smile plastered on my lips. "The cabin is furnished with everything Dr. Kizer has mentioned or you mentioned and more. It's the food and drink that you can either bring or it can be stocked." I take a deep breath. "Perhaps you have diet restrictions? And if you want anything particular that hasn't been mentioned, the number on the front can help."

"Do they...?" Mrs. Williams swallows. "...know our names?"

I shake my head. "No, ma'am. This is part of Dr. Kizer's therapy. It's completely confidential. I also wrote your ID number on the back. That is how they know you."

She nodded as she looked up at her husband with her eyes wide. "We should talk...about things. I read about something once..."

Mr. Williams stands taller. His action silences her words, yet by the gleam in his gaze, it's obvious that he's more than interested to hear her thoughts. Turning back to me, he nods. "Thank you, Marji. We'll see you and Dr. Kizer in two weeks."

"Bye." *Have a great time.* I don't say the last part, trying to squelch any images of their future before they take root in my mind.

As the door to the front office closes and the Williamses disappear, I lean back in my chair and exhale. I've been working here for over two years. You'd think those conversations would get easier.

"Marji?"

I turn as Dr. Ami Kizer steps from her office. In a gray pencil skirt, white silk blouse, and closed-toe high-heel pumps, no one would know that this proper lady spends her days discussing and encouraging sexual exploration.

"Yes?"

"Can you please close up? I have to leave early."

"Sure thing. Do you need today's notes transcribed tonight?"

"No," she says with a wave of her hand. "I have them all recorded. They can wait until tomorrow. You deserve to enjoy your night like everyone else."

Like everyone else.

"Okay."

"Is everything all right, Marji?"

I force a smile. "I'm your office manager, remember? I'm not a client."

"No, but you're also a friend. I couldn't keep this place running without you. If you ever want to talk..."

"I'm not exactly eligible for couples counseling." I make a scrunched face. "I'm minus the part about a couple."

Dr. Kizer shrugged. "The world is filled with halves of couples waiting to find one another. It's a matter of looking in the right place."

"And where would that be?" I ask.

"Sometimes where you least expect it. Have a good night, Marji."

"You too, Dr. Kizer. See you tomorrow."

WHAT TO DO NOW

LEND IT: Did you enjoy UNDENIABLE? Do you have a friend who'd enjoy UNDENIABLE? UNDENIABLE may be lent one time. Sharing is caring!

RECOMMEND IT: Do you have multiple friends who'd enjoy this short, steamy story? Tell them about it! Call, text, post, tweet...your recommendation is the nicest gift you can give to an author!

REVIEW IT: Tell the world. Please go to the retailer where you purchased this book, as well as Goodreads, and write a review. Please share your thoughts about UNDENIABLE on:

*Amazon, UNDENIABLE Customer Reviews

*Barnes & Noble, UNDENIABLE, Customer Reviews

*iBooks, UNDENIABLE Customer Reviews

* BookBub, UNDENIABLE Customer Reviews

*Goodreads.com/Aleatha Romig

BOOKS BY NEW YORK TIMES BESTSELLING AUTHOR ALEATHA ROMIG

THE SPARROW WEBS:

DANGEROUS WEB:

DUSK

Releasing September 29, 2020

DARK

Releasing November 10, 2020

DAWN

Releasing December 22, 2020

WEB OF DESIRE:

SPARK

Releasing January 14, 2020

FLAME

Releasing February 25, 2020

ASHES

Releasing April 7, 2020

TANGLED WEB:

TWISTED

Released May, 2019

OBSESSED

Released July, 2019

BOUND

Released August, 2019

WEB OF SIN:

SECRETS

Released October, 2018

LIES

Released December, 2018

PROMISES

Released January, 2019

THE INFIDELITY SERIES:

BETRAYAL

Book #1

Released October 2015

CUNNING

Book #2

Released January 2016

DECEPTION

Book #3

Released May 2016

ENTRAPMENT

Book #4

Released September 2016

FIDELITY

Book #5

Released January 2017

THE CONSEQUENCES SERIES:

CONSEQUENCES

(Book #1)

Released August 2011

TRUTH

(Book #2)

Released October 2012

CONVICTED

(Book #3)

Released October 2013

REVEALED

(Book #4)

Previously titled: Behind His Eyes Convicted: The Missing Years

Re-released June 2014

BEYOND THE CONSEQUENCES

(Book #5)

Released January 2015

RIPPLES

Released October 2017

CONSEQUENCES COMPANION READS:

BEHIND HIS EYES-CONSEQUENCES

Released January 2014

BEHIND HIS EYES-TRUTH

Released March 2014

STAND ALONE MAFIA THRILLER:

PRICE OF HONOR

Available Now

THE LIGHT DUET:

Published through Thomas and Mercer Amazon exclusive

INTO THE LIGHT

Released June, 2016

AWAY FROM THE DARK

Released October, 2016

TALES FROM THE DARK SIDE SERIES:

INSIDIOUS

(All books in this series are stand-alone erotic thrillers)

Released October 2014

INDULGENCE SERIES:

UNEXPECTED

Released August, 2018

UNCONVENTIONAL

Released January, 2018

UNFORGETTABLE

Released October, 2019

UNDENIABLE

Coming late summer 2020

ALEATHA'S LIGHTER ONES:

PLUS ONE

Stand-alone fun, sexy romance

Released May 2017

A SECRET ONE

A novella prequel to Another One

Released April 2018

ANOTHER ONE

Stand-alone fun, sexy romance

Released May 2018

ONE NIGHT

Stand-alone, sexy contemporary romance

September 2017

ABOUT THE AUTHOR

Aleatha Romig is a New York Times, Wall Street Journal, and USA Today bestselling author who lives in Indiana, USA. She has raised three children with her high school sweetheart and husband of over thirty years. Before she became a full-time author, she worked days as a dental hygienist and spent her nights writing. Now, when she's not imagining mind-blowing twists and turns, she likes to spend her time with her family and friends. Her other pastimes include reading and creating heroes/anti-heroes who haunt your dreams!

Aleatha impresses with her versatility in writing. She released her first novel, CONSEQUENCES, in August of 2011. CONSEQUENCES, a dark romance, became a bestselling series with five novels and two companions released from 2011 through 2015. The compelling and epic story of Anthony and Claire Rawlings has graced more than half a million e-readers. Her first stand-alone smart, sexy thriller INSIDIOUS was next. Then Aleatha released the five-novel INFIDELITY series, a romantic suspense saga, that took the reading world by storm, the final book landing on three of the top bestseller lists. She ventured into traditional publishing with Thomas and Mercer. Her books INTO THE LIGHT and AWAY FROM THE DARK were published through this mystery/thriller publisher in 2016.

In the spring of 2017, Aleatha again ventured into a different genre with her fun and sexy stand-alone romantic comedies with the USA Today bestseller PLUS ONE. She continued with ONE NIGHT and ANOTHER ONE.

If you like fun, sexy, novellas that make your heart pound, try her UNCONVENTIONAL, UNEXPECTED, and UNFORGETTABLE.

In 2018 Aleatha returned to her dark romance roots with the dangerous romance of the Sparrow Webs. WEB OF SIN, TANGLED WEB, and WEB OF DESIRE.

Aleatha is a "Published Author's Network" member of the Romance Writers of America, NINC, and PEN America. She is represented by Kevan Lyon of Marsal Lyon Literary Agency.

facebook.com/aleatharomig
twitter.com/aleatharomig
instagram.com/aleatharomig

Made in the USA
Monee, IL
06 June 2021